SHIFTING
PARADIGMS

SHIFTING PARADIGMS

DANIELLE FORREST

The Eternal Scribe Publishing
Indianapolis, IN

PRONUNCIATIONS

- Kou - Coo
- Surg - Surge
- Diehli - Day-lee
- Hacht - Hacked
- Ateles - Ah-tell-ease
- Taln - Talon
- Eirse - Air-see
- Danaus - Duh-nos

FOREWORD

Hello, friend!

In this novel, the main character, Victoria, is an undiagnosed autistic woman. I've done my best to avoid common (and harmful) stereotypes like you'll see in Rain Man, Music, and The Good Doctor, as well as attempting to clearly indicate good and bad approaches for interacting with an autistic person.

These are, of course, not exhaustive, and if you would like other resources, I would recommend Yo Samdy Sam, an autistic YouTuber, or ASAN (Autistic Self Advocacy Network).

At all costs, do **not** consult resources coming from Autism Speaks, as many see the organization as a hate group focused on autistic children. In the past, they have created campaigns featuring the following themes: autism will destroy your marriage, autism will bankrupt you, and parents fantasizing about killing their autistic children.

With that awfulness set aside, I hope you enjoy the book!

PROLOGUE

*V*ictoria crossed her ship excitedly, shaking out her hands in an attempt to dispel some of the excess energy. She'd had a breakthrough recently in her research. It was fantastic, something truly revolutionary. She wanted to tell someone, but she knew how that would end. It always ended one of two ways. Either a person's eyes would glaze over as she waxed poetic about spaceships, mechanical engineering, and advanced physics principles, or they would try to take advantage.

Most people did the latter, which was why she had so few friends. Really, just three. She walked into her bedroom. Dirty and clean clothes were piled next to each other, her bed had never been made since the day she moved in, and it looked like she'd forgotten to clean up after breakfast again. A plate sat on the table, a half-eaten steamed pork bun looking dry and hard on its white surface. Next to it, a cup was half-filled with what was likely *very* cold tea. The cup was one of her favorites, an unusual piece she'd picked up on her first trip to an alien market.

And now that she was thinking about food, she realized she'd forgotten to eat lunch. Her stomach gnawed at her, as if to reinforce that realization.

She turned her back on the dirty dishes, moving to her desk, which was drowning in miscellaneous *stuff*. She walked to it, throwing her sweatshirt on the back of her chair, closing the notebook that had a pen sitting across it, tip clicked out. Her tablet sat half underneath the notebook, screen still powered on, but almost dead since she'd left for her lab hours ago. She dropped it on the magnetic charger, frowning at the mess before her.

She didn't like messes; they tended to make her head feel cluttered, chaotic, cloudy. Unfortunately, she couldn't seem to help herself. No matter how hard she tried, she just couldn't seem to keep herself organized. Angus, the ship's AI, helped. Actually, he helped a lot. He reminded her to eat, to take showers, to make trips planetside to get supplies when they were running low. Without him, God only knew how she would end up.

"You were going to contact Jessie and Cass," the AI said, his simulated Scottish brogue strong. It had taken her a while to get used to his accent, but now she even responded to him with a similar accent sometimes. It probably didn't help that she rarely spoke to anyone else.

"The comm?" Angus said, prompting her again.

"Right." She shook her head, shaking out her hands for good measure before sitting at her desk. She supposed she could have set up a comm in her lab. After all, she'd *built* the ship, designed it. She could have done whatever she wanted, but just the idea sent anxiety spiking through her. "Okay, call them," she said before chickening out.

Wait, why was she calling them again? She looked down and over, opening her notebook once more. Maybe she'd left herself a note. Bold letters jumped out at her. "This might work. Should try today."

Right!

A smile crossed her face and the excited energy she'd been feeling returned, washing away the anxiety of making a call.

"Hi, Victoria!" Jess said through the comm.

Victoria jerked her head up, gaze shifting to the screen on the wall just beyond her desk. Technically, the entire wall was a screen, but right now, only a section directly in front of her desk lit up with an image of the *Trojan*'s cockpit. "Oh, good, the call went through."

Jessie grinned. "Did you think it wouldn't?"

Victoria shrugged, her excitement bubbling up once more. "I wasn't really paying attention."

"What's got you so excited? No, wait." Jess turned around and yelled. "Cass! Kou! Victoria's on the line!"

Victoria wanted to get up and pace, finding it hard to sit still. That happened sometimes. She'd found over the years that noise canceling headphones playing instrumental music helped, but she couldn't do that on a call.

On the screen, Cass stomped into the room at her younger sister's back. Jessie looked behind her and laughed.

Victoria squinted and leaned forward, trying to figure out what had made Jessie laugh, but she'd never been great with social cues, and the stupid comm screen gave hardly any detail. She kind of hated video calls, but what other options were there?

3

"Fly's undone," Jessie said, still looking toward the door at the back of the cockpit.

Which was when Victoria noticed the dark shape of Kou, Cass's boyfriend. He flinched, looking down and reaching for his crotch.

Jessie turned around. "Okay, we're all here. What's got you so excited, Victoria?"

She thought back to that moment in the lab, the moment everything had come together. It had been so beautiful, perfect. It seemed so elegant in retrospect. Victoria couldn't wait to get started working again, but her stomach growled again. She needed a break. She would work better if she got some sleep and a shower, too.

"I had a breakthrough." She shook her head, her hands waving in the air, her excitement getting the better of her. "It's big. Really big. This could very well change the way we look at space travel." She wanted to tell them, tell the world even, but she couldn't, not the least of which because neither Jessie nor Cass would understand a word of it.

"Really?" Jessie leaned forward, Cass and Kou moving closer to the camera behind her.

She nodded. "Uh huh. I've been working on this for so long, I can't believe I'm there. I still need to do some testing, but I think it's just a formality." God, she couldn't wait to get started on the testing. She started planning out how to test her calculations. Parts lists started building in her head, but she had to stop herself. If she didn't, she would get lost in her own thoughts again, and she couldn't afford to do that right now. She was on a call.

"You're not really going to leave us hanging there, are you, Vicky?" Cass said behind her sister, her weight pressing down on the back of Jessie's chair. "That's just mean."

Victoria laughed. "No, I'll tell you." She shook her head. "God, this is just…" Unbelievable.

Overhead, Angus's voice interrupted her. "The communications channel has been compromised."

Victoria flinched, eyes widening, panic flaring up like a tsunami inside her. "I have to go. Sorry." Reaching forward, she cut the connection.

She looked up at the ceiling, jumping to her feet so quickly she nearly knocked her chair over. "Angus, what the heck was that?"

"As I said, the communications channel was compromised."

Victoria ground her teeth, wanting to pull at her hair. She hated when he talked like that. "Angus!"

"Someone may have been listening in on the call."

Chills ran up her arms and spine, and she froze in place, her mind going blank as the implications settled in.

Someone was listening in.

There was only one reason she could think of why someone would want to listen in on her comms.

Somehow, someone had figured out what she was working on…

And they wanted it.

CHAPTER ONE

*S*urg sat in his office, staring at his computer screen. He should be working. There were financials to go over, projects to approve. There was always work to be done, money to be made. Sometimes, though, his office felt more like a prison than a palace. He had all the finest things, all the best equipment. Every item in his office was either a status symbol or functional but top of the line.

He could have done without the status symbols, but it was expected. After all, he *was* owner of Inia Intergalactic, an enormous company with a lot of money and even more clout. There was a certain image in people's heads when they first arrived in his domain, one he had to maintain.

Still, it didn't stop him from wanting to escape from time to time.

He looked over at his comm. *I wonder what my brother's doing.* He was tempted to call him, but Varn was probably busy. The two of them were always working, which was why they hadn't spoken in so long, and it'd been even longer since they'd talked about something other than business.

As he reached for the display to pull up the directory, it chirped and flashed an alert. "Incoming call from the *Trojan*," the screen said, with symbols under it to accept or send to the messaging system. He hit accept.

"Inia, sir," Cass said, nodding at him.

"Surg, please," he said, frowning as he noted the worry on her face. The normally laid back privateer seemed tense, her posture slightly hunched and leaning toward the screen. "Is everything all right?"

Cass ran a hand through her purple hair as she took a deep breath. "I'm not sure."

"Well, tell me. Maybe I can help." He rested his forearms on the hard surface of his desk, leaning forward unconsciously. The warm elegance of his office served a strong contrast against the gray cockpit behind Cass on screen.

"It's a friend of ours, Victoria. I think something's wrong. I just don't know what."

"Why do you think something's wrong?"

She leaned back, looking off to the side. "It started with a comm. She cut it off abruptly."

"Is that not normal, then?"

She shook her head, then frowned and nodded. "Yes and no. Victoria can be blunt and a bit absentminded. She's definitely hung up on us before, but this was different. She looked... she looked almost scared. And the AI said something in the background." She closed her eyes. "Angus, what did he say? Did you record it?"

"Aye. Her AI said the comm was compromised."

Compromised? "Is your friend a pirate like yourself?"

Cass snorted, the first trace of humor entering her face since the call began. "Victoria? A pirate?" She laughed. "No. She's a scientist. Now that I think about it, though, she was really excited about something." She shook her head. "It doesn't make any sense. It's been too long for it to be nothing, but it can't be foul play. It just can't."

She sighed, leaning back in a sprawl against her seat. "And yet, we haven't been able to get in contact with her since."

"How long has it been?"

She leaned forward. "Weeks. I know she's not the most communicative. I mean, if she gets absorbed in her work, she could get consumed by it for days, but this isn't like her." She shook her head. "No matter what she's doing in her lab, we would have heard from her by now. Something's wrong."

"Have you tried tracking her ship?"

"Yeah. I'm not getting any pingbacks. It doesn't make any sense. Our ships are identical, so in theory I should be able to just ping the AI. They're designed for that, but it's not working. Neither is the tracker I installed on her ship. If nothing else, *that* should give me precise coordinates, but nothing. It's like we're being blocked."

He nodded. That certainly sounded ominous. His mind came up with a wide variety of scenarios, none of them good. He didn't know this Victoria person, but he knew Cass. She was a good person and an even better contractor. It sounded like her friend was an innocent, and in a lot of trouble. "So, how can I help?"

"You… have connections I don't. I'm really worried about her. She'd not a pirate like me or a cargo ship captain like our friend, Ellie. She's not a fighter. She can't defend herself."

He nodded. "Okay. I'll send out some feelers and get back to you as soon as I know something."

Cass sighed. "Thank you."

Victoria felt like her skin was going to crawl off. Grease covered her arms from the equipment, something sharp was digging into her hip, and these coveralls were irritating her skin to the point of distraction.

She leaned back from the series of circuit boards and wires in front of her, trying to stretch out a kink in her back. "Angus, add more comfortable coveralls to my shopping list."

"Done."

"Thanks, Angus." She reached in, isolated the circuit she'd been looking for, then shimmied out of the wall. A part of her wanted to set everything to rights. She hated seeing her baby like this. Panels leaned against the walls, wires were pulled out of their once neat bundles, and tools were strewn about in a chaotic mess that made her head spin. "Okay, what about now?"

"Nothing."

"Dang it," she said, flailing her arms several times, her jaw tense. Victoria stood up and paced the corridor, taking deep breaths to calm the episode she felt rearing up with alarming speed. She didn't need to lose her shit right now. She needed to fix this.

Why couldn't she figure this out? It was her own ship, for crying out loud! She'd designed the thing, but she still couldn't figure out how someone had compromised her comms.

Or how they knew about her research, for that matter. She hadn't even started any experiments yet, and it had been weeks since the comm breach. Which was probably making her stress worse, actually. She was always a bit calmer and put together when she was designing or building. She'd always loved spaceships and all the technology that went along with them. So, designing ships and improving their technologies was a passion of hers, one she happily indulged.

Unfortunately, she knew someone had compromised her ship, her baby. But no matter how hard she looked, she couldn't figure out what they'd done. Angus had detected the outgoing signal, but they hadn't been able to trace the signal back to its source code. In fact, the damned thing had run a military-grade wipe to clear the history of the comm. They knew absolutely nothing.

She stopped and banged her head against the wall. "God, why didn't I become a computer programmer?" She could do some programming, especially converting her mathematical equations into computer algorithms, but she usually needed Cass to help with turning her barebones code into a more useful program.

More importantly, Victoria's code always started from the tech side. She could develop code to complement the hardware she designed, but staring at another person's code made her confused, scrambled.

"You shouldn't hit yourself, Victoria."

She sighed, looking up at the plain metal ceiling. "I know that, Angus." Frankly, it hadn't even hurt. She rubbed her forehead and started pacing again.

They'd disconnected every system that was designed to send signals off ship. It bought them time to find the problem, but every diagnostic was coming up empty.

Could they have compromised Angus's programing? If they did, they could simply make him ignore their code, and Victoria didn't have the expertise to figure it out. She stopped her hand, realizing she was rubbing and scratching her chest above the neckline of her coveralls.

"Man, I wish Cass were here." Should she call her? Maybe Cass could find the issue?

She turned and leaned against the wall, her anxiety getting the better of her once more, like a thousand bees crawling over her skin while her stomach churned endlessly.

She took another deep breath.

What more could she do? "Angus, how long was the signal? How much could have been sent?"

"Unknown. Depends on systems affected."

Of course. If they had access to navigation, they could send her location. Which was why she hadn't stopped moving since shutting down all outbound signals.

Victoria huffed in frustration. She was stuck, frozen in limbo. She couldn't return to normal, but neither could she solve the problem. "Angus, how much longer until you finish the line-by-line code analysis?"

"Another week."

Crap. "Okay, what else can I do? What else can I check?" She might not be much of a programmer, but she knew this ship like the back of her hand. If anyone could find a bug or transmitter on it, she could.

But she feared she was running out of time.

And she knew she was running out of supplies…

CHAPTER TWO

Surg had gathered a team to look for Cass's friend, Victoria, but the woman was a ghost. She never stopped moving, and it was hard chasing down likely information on her whereabouts. There had been several reports of ships detecting anomalies, but that didn't give much to go by. Often it was a ship sending no outbound signals, but still registering as an object to avoid. This created a technical error in the navigation system. One set of sensors said there was a ship, while another said there was nothing there. Usually, those types of errors happened with stealth ships. In all these reports, though, the sensors picked up on the material the ship was created from, which meant something else was going on. He was almost positive it was her.

He had the team tracking down these error reports, but he didn't hold a lot of hope of them finding her that way. There was so little data.

Surg stepped from his ship onto the dusty ground of the dockyard. He didn't expect this hunch to pan out, but he didn't know what else to do. Honestly, it was a bit of wild speculation on his part. While over the last week or so, her movements, assuming they *were* her movements, had seemed erratic, the last few data points had been leading in this general direction. When he'd done a search of the system, this was the only likely place someone might go. It was a medium-sized space port. People often came here either to find work or resupply.

He wondered if he was imagining things, drawing conclusions and patterns where they didn't exist. He hadn't been willing to take his team off real leads to follow this, so he'd decided to go alone. Going alone also had the added benefit that he wouldn't look like an idiot when he was proved wrong.

Around him, most everyone was dusty or dirty. Loud voices and the occasional engine filled the air, leaving little room for thought. To his left, a greasy man was working on a ship, a panel leaning precariously against its hull. His tool scraped against the metal, making Surg flinch. Shifting his attention, he looked for the Port Master. Hopefully, he would have records of ships that had landed here recently.

Surg jogged forward, dodging bodies as he crossed the busy yard. "Excuse me, sir?"

A chubby man with orange skin turned, his coveralls stretched tight over his girth. "What do you want?"

He rubbed his fingers together. "Looking for some information."

"How much is it worth to ya'?"

Surg pulled out his comm and showed the screen where a transfer authorization spoke for him.

The Port Master nodded, but didn't smile. "What do you want?"

"I'm looking for an Earth ship that might have come here."

"Earth, huh?" He pulled a tablet off his hip. "Don't get many of those out this way. Let's see." His thick fingers moved over the screen as he hummed to himself, seemingly unconsciously. "Yeah, we got an Earth ship in port. The…" He frowned. "I really need to update the language processor on this thing. It always screws up when adapting non-native alphabets. I think this might be Disco Very? Does that make sense?"

He didn't recognize the ship's name. Certainly, it wasn't in Usan. But then, why would it have been? "Do you know the owner's name?"

"One moment." He scrolled down and shook his head. "Another foreign word. Vick Tor E A?"

Surg blinked. It took him a moment to fit the pieces together. Victoria. "Yes, that's her."

"Well, she's still in port, according to the records."

"What?! No, sorry. Thank you."

She was still here. He hadn't expected that. But where could she be? He glanced around him, but there were too many ships to pick out hers without roaming around. Once he saw it, he was sure he would recognize it. Cass had said her ship was identical to Victoria's, and he still had recordings of her ship docking with his station. He'd used that data to help him track Victoria down.

Surg just couldn't believe it had actually worked. He couldn't believe she was here. Should he look for her or her ship? But as he glanced around, he nixed the idea of looking for her. She could be anywhere. The dockyard was busy, but it was nothing in comparison to the market. As he hovered at the entrance, he saw nothing but a sea of bodies bumping into each other, pressed together so tightly that nothing could squeeze past. He would never find her in that mess.

Surg turned around. The dockyard was large, with smaller ships and shuttles close to the market and larger ships at the periphery. Victoria's ship was somewhat small, certainly smaller than the behemoths in the background. Hopefully, her ship was near the market and he could find it quickly and wait for her to return.

He weaved around small groups, chatting animatedly or walking with purpose. Able to see the ships closest to the market, he walked between two shuttles, ducking under the wing of one as he made his way to the next ring of ships. On the other side, peeking around the rear thrusters of the shuttles, the dusty, dirty yard continued, but it was less crowded.

He stepped out at a brisk walk, leaning to check between ships as he went, searching for hers. Urgency drove him, but he forced himself to take his time. He didn't want to miss her, but he would hear a ship taking off. He could easily look up and visually confirm whether a ship leaving was hers. And if it was, he could give chase. It would be fine.

He was just starting to settle into his task when a streak rushed across the path in front of him, disappearing between two small ships to his left.

"What the…" It took his mind a moment to process what he'd seen. The being had been small, with long hair flying out behind.

I wonder why they were running…

Then he got his answer. A big bastard stormed after the runner, a murderous look on his face. Surg's jaw dropped. The chaser also disappeared between the ships. For a moment, he just stood there, his mind unusually slow to respond.

"Screw it," he said, rushing after the two.

Victoria hated going planetside. It always involved people. She had a hard enough time understanding humans. Most aliens were completely beyond her capability.

Not to mention, it always involved negotiating. Victoria sucked at negotiating. She invariably walked away feeling like she'd been taken advantage of.

She wished market vendors would just tell her a price and be done with it. Why did they have to make it so complicated? She just wanted to resupply and get the hell out of Dodge.

It didn't help that she felt certain she was being followed. She looked behind her, scanning the crowd for threats, but there were too many people and too much chaos. She hefted her bag a little higher on her shoulder. The messenger bag's strap dug hard between her breasts, making her look a little ridiculous, but she'd never cared much for appearances.

She started turning back around, and suddenly, her shoulder bumped into something.

"Hey, watch it!" an angry voice said.

She spun toward the voice. "Sorry." Her heart pounded in her chest, making her feel shaky. An alien man stomped away, grumbling under his breath. She stood in the middle of the street, looking around. Nothing seemed out of place. And yet still, the feeling wouldn't leave her. "There's nothing there."

No one's following you.

But she didn't really know that, and the unknown was fraying her nerves. At the moment, Angus was all but useless. They'd killed all signal transmission, which limited his abilities. It left her constantly wondering, because she didn't *know* if they were being followed. There was no *way* to know. The entire time she'd been on this planet, that thought had made her skin crawl. She just wanted to get back to the *Discovery* and disappear again.

As she thought of her ship, her frustration returned with a vengeance. She *still* had no idea what was going on. She didn't know how they'd infiltrated her ship, how they'd sent that signal, or what their next move might be. It left her feeling like an idiot. This was *her* ship, *her* baby. How could anyone do this to the *Discovery* without her knowing, without her being able to fix it? She knew every inch of that ship, for crying out loud!

So why can't I figure this out? Why is this so hard?

Unfortunately, not everything could be solved with logic. Most people didn't operate that way. She paused. Maybe she *should* call in Cass for help. Cass was a pirate as well as a programmer. She was smart, but also savvy, street smart. Cass could take care of herself in a way that she never could.

Victoria rubbed her chest as she left the market, trying to decide on her next course of action. The vendors were delivering her supplies to the ship. In fact, they should have already loaded everything up by the time she got there. A part of her cringed at the idea of someone else on her ship, especially when she wasn't there to watch them, but it was pretty common practice. Many ships came to these markets to resupply, and no vendor wanted their delivery boys to wait around for the buyer to return to their ship. It could take all day. They drove supplies out to the ships using the roads behind the stalls and dropped off the goods.

The smart buyers had guest codes to their cargo area, like valet keys in reverse. When she'd customized the cargo area of her ship to be a lab, she'd left a storage area at the back that could be accessed with a guest code. It gave her peace of mind for the most part, but sometimes she still got anxious.

She stepped out of the market and into the more crowded area of the dockyard, her messenger bag smacking repetitively against her butt and upper thighs as she walked. The urge to look behind her rose once again, and she couldn't resist. She turned. One "man" stood out, a big alien with a wicked, cruel scowl that left her feeling chilled. For a moment, she couldn't look away, transfixed with a sort of instinctual terror.

She was used to being afraid. She was always afraid, really, except when she was in her lab. The whole world, the whole galaxy, was terrifying if you really thought about it. Which was probably why it took so little for her fight-or-flight response to kick in.

Like it did now, with a vengeance. She didn't know who he was, what he wanted, or even if he was looking at her. Victoria didn't know if she even registered in the larger canvas of faces in the crowd, but it took all her effort not to run, not to react. Turning forward once again, she pushed the reaction down, shoving it as deep as she could. Unfortunately, it was like compressing a spring. She could feel the pressure, the effort it took to keep all of that down.

Victoria had reached the nose of one of the first ships when she felt compelled to turn around again. She couldn't say why she'd done it. Maybe the pressure had become too much. Maybe she'd just wanted reassurance. Or maybe some deeper instinct had sensed it before her conscious mind could catch up. Still, she turned slowly, some part of her knowing what she would find. And there, right behind her, was the man from before, the angry, scary man. He was looking straight at her. She froze, her mind going blank, her muscles rigid. The world around her dimmed for a moment. For that brief spell, she couldn't hear the overloud crowd or see the movement of the people around her. Her vision became blurry.

Then everything snapped into focus. Noise became so loud she wanted to clap her hands to her ears, and she was momentarily disoriented by the movement around her. Her brain didn't want to kick into gear, and she felt the need to act, but couldn't figure out what to do. She stepped backward. Looking up, she spotted the scary guy again, and she reacted on instinct, turning and fleeing as fast as her, admittedly clumsy, legs could carry her.

She dashed between the two ships nearest her. After a few steps, she could hear him behind her. He'd cleared the crowd, his breathing harsh in the less chaotic environment. She passed between the first ships, running down the path between them and straight toward the lineup of parked spaceships. The *Discovery* wasn't far, just past this row and then a few ships down to the right.

Her heart pounded, blotting out the sound around her. She pushed herself harder, her muscles burning with the unaccustomed activity. As she cleared the nose of the next ship, she tripped on a rock, her arms flailing as she struggled to keep going without falling. The rock pinged loudly against the hull of a ship, and she recovered her momentum after a few steps.

Victoria turned, her hand skimmed over the smooth, cool metal of a rear thruster housing as she aimed at her ship. It was in sight now. She smiled, seeing salvation within her grasp. No one else was on the path ahead of her.

Then a grunt came from behind her, and her hair was pulled hard, her scalp screaming in protest. She fell backward, reaching for her ponytail, but he just yanked her again, sending her falling back against a hard chest. She scrambled to get her feet under her, then he wrapped his meaty fingers around her throat. A croak escaped her, but the rest was cut off as he squeezed. Her hands detoured, reaching for his hand where it squeezed tight, but it was like a mouse trying to dislodge a cat. Her fingernails scratched against his skin ineffectually.

My God, I'm going to die.

"Hey, stop!" a male voice said, coming from behind.

Her attacker shifted behind her, and a gunshot went off. She flinched, the sound hurting her ears, deafening her for moments afterward. Time distorted, then she was released. She dropped to the ground, her bones like noodles.

Someone grabbed her arms, moving her to face him. She looked up, her abused neck protesting the movement. It wasn't her attacker. It must have been the one who'd intervened.

"Are you okay?"

His words sounded a little muffled, but she understood. She nodded, her throat already feeling tender and swollen from being manhandled.

He pulled up on her arms, helping her stand. "Which ship is yours?"

She waved her hand, pointing in the general direction. He helped her forward, his movements slow.

Then, after her heart had finally dropped off to a more silent tempo, another gunshot broke the silence.

"Beffa!" he said, grabbing her hand and yanking her toward the ship. His other arm rose, a pistol at the end of it, and he returned fire. A constant barrage of gunfire serenaded them as he pushed her toward the access panel of the ship. "Quick. I've got him pinned down, but we're easy targets here."

She nodded, trying to block out the sound of the battlefield around her. It made her hearing distort, causing a headache to

21

bloom between her temples. "Angus, open up." A moment later, the door they'd approached hissed and popped open. Victoria slipped through, dragging her savior with her by the back of his shirt. He continued to fire up until the moment the door closed. "Angus, engage all locks and prepare for departure."

Her guest looked over at her, his gun arm falling to his side. He was grungy, wearing clothes coated in a layer of dust. His head was covered in wild, thick hair, with two pointed ears sticking out near the top.

I wonder what they feels like.

She shook herself, trying not to think about it.

He tapped the gun against his leg, looking away from her. "Well, this wasn't how I expected the day to go." He laughed, the almost howling noise drawing her gaze to his slightly elongated jaw.

She turned away, and the inner door opened automatically. In the background, the engines started up, the noise subtle but noticeable to her after so long aboard. "Come on. We've got to get strapped in. Angus is preparing for launch, but we can't be standing around when we take off."

"Right." His boots cracked against the floor plates, loud and jarring in her normally quiet ship. She didn't like it. She tried to ignore it, pretend he wasn't there, but she could feel his presence at her back, like a looming threat, though she wasn't afraid of him.

Which was stupid. She had no reason to trust him. She didn't *know* him. Hell, she didn't even know his name. He could be anyone. For all she knew, he could have been listening in on her comms. He could have been following her all this time. Maybe he'd even planned that whole attack to get to her.

In the end, it didn't matter. She needed to get off the ground, and the question of his motives was a problem for another time. She picked up speed, rushing to get the ship off the ground. The loose panels and tools that had littered the hallway were gone, cleared away before landing. Within moments, she slipped into the cockpit and dropped into her seat. The chair groaned under the sudden weight, and she ignored it, pulling the straps over her shoulders. She hated these straps, but when designing the ship, she'd simply been unable to find anything better. As she clipped everything in place, the straps dug into the sides of her neck, which was even more sensitive than usual because of the attack.

She looked over at her guest, her apparent hero. "We're ready, Angus."

"Hold tight."

The ship lifted vertically, pushing off in a dust cloud that consumed their surroundings. Once they cleared the other ships, she was slammed into the back of her seat as the ship surged forward, the engines quiet as a breeze as they approached outer space.

Finally, the force eased and Victoria took a single, calming breath. It didn't quite help. Her throat was scraped raw, pain slicing through her as she took the breath, abruptly ending her attempt at controlling her emotions.

After several careful, shallow breaths, she unbuckled her harness and turned to the man beside her. "So… you're hurt!" She jumped to her feet, panic rising through her. Blood bloomed in a circle on the upper sleeve of his shirt. All she could see was that red. Was it growing? Was he going to bleed out? Was that the prize he would win for helping her?

Was he going to die?

He looked down, as if only now having noticed his injury. "Huh…"

Victoria shook herself, steeling her nerves. "Come on." She reached out an arm. "Let's get you fixed up."

CHAPTER THREE

Surg lay on the table in the med bay as the automated system worked on his arm. He hadn't even felt it as the bullet struck him. All he'd been thinking about was protecting the woman on the path, the woman who now paced the edge of the room, rubbing her chest.

In the thick of the action, he'd noticed exactly nothing about her. Laying there, he couldn't say what her ship looked like, but he was fairly certain she was a human like Cass. In fact, she could actually be the woman he was looking for. What were the chances he would encounter another human on that planet?

And while Cass's description hadn't been very detailed, she certainly fit. Black hair, shorter and heavier than Cass. It could be her.

The AI started to bandage his arm, the material pulling tight to his skin. He sighed. The pressure felt good, alleviating some of the pain. The woman turned to him, her hand still pressed near her throat, and spoke. "I'm so sorry I got you involved in this. I can't believe this is happening. This shouldn't be happening." She made an aborted movement, like she was about to start pacing again, and stopped.

Surg sat up as the robotic arm completed its task. "You didn't get me involved in anything. I'm the one that leapt to the rescue. You can't control someone else's actions." He hopped off the bed, reaching out a hand. "I'm Inia Surg, by the way. You can call me Surg."

She hesitated for a moment before taking his hand. Did he mess it up? He'd read that gripping a human's hand and shaking it briefly up and down was a standard greeting. Was he wrong? He wracked his brain. He'd used his right hand, offered it with palm faced left. What had he missed?

She shook his hand up and down twice, then pulled back, rubbing her palm against her pant leg, not meeting his eyes. "Victoria Chan."

So, she *was* the woman he was looking for. "It's a pleasure to meet you, Victoria. Actually, by some weird twist of fate, I was actually looking for you."

She stiffened and jerked backward, her back hitting the wall with a dull thud. She looked up at him, appearing terrified.

"Easy." He tried to calm her. "Cass sent me. She's been looking for you."

Victoria relaxed, but didn't pull away from the wall. "She did?" Her voice was small, quiet. Her gaze darted to the open doorway to her left.

"Oh, yes. She got worried after that last communication ended so abruptly. When she couldn't contact you after that, she started looking for you. And when that didn't pan out, she asked for my help. I think of her as a friend, so..." He shrugged.

She nodded, but looked like she was ready to flee.

He pointed at her neck. "Maybe you should get that checked out. It's already bruising."

She touched the darkening marks, her fingers shaking a little. "It'll be fine. Just some bruises."

"Okay." Silence fell between them. He didn't know what to say, what to do. Clearly, she was scared, and he didn't think it was just because of the attack today. He suspected there was something she wasn't saying, a reason behind *all* her recent behaviors. But what? Was it something he could help with? *Did* he want to help? He'd agreed to look for her. That was it. He'd found her, so technically, his job was done.

But now? Standing in front of her after she'd been attacked, after seeing how scared she was? He couldn't just do nothing. But what could he do? He didn't know what was wrong, and she didn't seem inclined to trust him. He could understand that. She'd been chased, attacked, and there was something else going on. He could certainly understand her being wary of strangers.

Surg just needed her to stop seeing him as one. He needed to get her comfortable with him. He leaned back against the bed, keeping his body language open. She seemed to distance herself when stressed, so he would give her whatever space she needed. "Let me help you," he blurted.

"What?" She jerked her head up, startled out of her thoughts.

"Let me help you. I don't know what's wrong, but clearly something is. Cass said you're a scientist, that you're not a fighter." He chuckled. "I'm certainly not a pirate like your friend, but I've got some skills. Just tell me what's wrong. We can figure it out together."

She shook her head, her hands reaching up to rub at her temples. "I can't deal with this right now." Her voice was shaky, and she closed her eyes near the end.

"Well, why don't you get some sleep? We can talk when you wake up."

She stared at him, distrust in her eyes. She didn't make a move.

"I can stay here." He patted the bed at his back. "I've slept on worse." That didn't seem to encourage her. "You can even lock me in, if you like."

Her shoulders dropped fractionally, and she nodded and left. The door closed behind her, the lock seemingly engaging automatically.

He let out a sigh and looked around. "Now, what do I do?"

Victoria felt exhausted. She rubbed her forehead. Her cool hands soothed the overheated skin there, but the grit from the dockyard felt like sandpaper, minimizing the effect. Her batteries were drained after everything that had happened. She wanted to just curl up and sleep, but she knew she couldn't, not without taking a shower. She was sweaty and covered in dust. If she didn't get cleaned up, her mind would scream a protest the moment she lay down.

Already, she could feel her skin crawling. She blindly walked to her bathroom, stripping the moment the door closed behind her. She flung garments, uncaring where they ended up, not really seeing her environment, though the constant hum around her was starting to get on her nerves.

The shower turned on as she stepped into the bathroom. *Thanks, Angus.* The words stuck in her throat, like a boulder had locked them in place. She stepped under the hot spray, letting it beat down on her, massaging away her thoughts, her problems. She loved taking showers, though she couldn't say why. The rest of the world just fell away, leaving only the heat, the pressure of the water pounding her skin, and the rush of the fake waterfall hitting her eardrums. There was nothing like it in the world.

Sometimes, she just wanted to live in her shower. Unfortunately, while her in-line water heater wouldn't run out, she lived on a spaceship. Eventually, she *would* run out of filtered water in the tanks. The filtration system was good, but that also meant it was a little slow, certainly slower than the water flow on the shower-head.

A little sad, Victoria turned off the water and grabbed a towel from a pile on the floor. She patted herself dry as she left the room, crossing to the drawers she kept her clothes in. As the towel ran over her neck, she was reminded of the attack she'd suffered so recently. She could almost *feel* the man strangling her, her airway cutoff. The fear. She stood there, not moving, just staring blindly at the dresser. Victoria could feel the hot pressure of the swelling afterward, the gritty feel of her sore throat. She rubbed the skin there, reminding herself that it was already starting to heal. The area was tender, but the swelling had already gone done, and by morning, there would be no traces of the attack except in her mind.

Shaking off the phantom sensations, Victoria opened a drawer and pulled out underwear from an assortment of unfolded garments. Every drawer was like that, holding clothes sorted by type, but otherwise a chaotic mess. She'd learned a long time ago that if laundry required folding or hanging, it would never quite make it to the drawers or closet. So, she bought her clothes carefully, avoiding anything that itched or clung for sensory reasons and anything that wrinkled for practical ones.

Semi-dressed, she turned around, dropping exhaustedly into her bed and curling up under the comforter. She cocooned herself inside the fluffy material, letting all her muscles ease, but her mind was a different story. She was too tired to think, but too wired to shut off her brain. Instead, it kept sending off half-started thoughts she couldn't follow through on.

I just need to sleep.

Her body seemed to melt into the material, but her mind just wouldn't stop. Each time her brain made a suggestion, coming up with new avenues for investigation, she squeezed her eyes more tightly closed.

Please, just let me sleep.

CHAPTER FOUR

$\mathcal{V}$ictoria woke up on her side, her mind groggy but feeling sharper than it had the night before. Her skin ached from sleeping in one position for too long, but that was nothing new. She pushed up and out of bed, rubbing her eyes as she stumbled to her feet. Unfortunately, her situation didn't seem any better in the light of day.

She wanted to return to her lab, put on a pair of noise canceling headphones, and just forget about everything for a while. She could lose herself for the rest of the day and not have to think about any of this. But that wouldn't solve her problems. She would still have a stranger locked in her med bay. She would still have the mystery to solve.

"Ugh," she groaned, dropping her head as she rubbed her forehead. "Why is this happening to me? I left Earth to avoid this crap. Why can't people just leave me alone?"

Victoria was not a people person, never had been. She was an introvert, liked being alone, never understood everyone's obsession with social interaction. She just found it exhausting. And she wasn't very good at it. She had a special gift for inadvertently insulting people. If she was *lucky*, she would realize she'd made a mistake immediately after the words slipped from her mouth. More often, though, she didn't have a clue.

So, what do I do with the guy in the med bay?

Her mind was just as blank on that subject as it was yesterday. Although, she supposed, she couldn't leave him in there. The room didn't have any food or bathroom facilities. She had to let him out sometime. She opened her mouth to ask Angus to release him, but her words wouldn't form.

But why? Why couldn't she say the words? What was stopping her from releasing him?

I don't trust him.

When she imagined him roaming her ship, her anxiety spiked. She didn't know him and wasn't even sure if Cass really had sent him. He could have been lying about that. After all, the compromised communication had been *with* Cass. Whoever was after her could have easily gotten her friend's information from that call.

Victoria continued to think as she pulled clothes on, trying to keep her mind focused on the task at hand. More than anything else, she needed to get her life back on track. That meant figuring out who'd bugged her comms, and presumably, who'd hired someone to attack her back on that planet. What had been the goal there? Kill her? Scare her? Kidnap her?

She shook her head. It could be any of those things. Or something she wasn't even considering. Like maybe that attack had been meant to endear her toward her "savior." After all, what better way to infiltrate her ship than by "rescuing" her.

She groaned, feeling defeated.

I shouldn't have brought him on board.

Surg woke with a crick in his neck. He wasn't lying when he'd said he'd slept on worse, but that was as a child, not as an adult with increasingly old bones. His whole body ached as he sat up, staring down at the hard, pillowless bed. He rolled his neck and stretched, trying to work out the various kinks that had settled in overnight.

He crossed the room and checked the door. Still locked. "Okay. Now what?" The med bay was a single room without closets or adjoining bathrooms. It held a single bed in the middle with lights and robotic arms above. Around the walls, cabinets and countertops filled the room, leaving almost no empty wall space. He was tempted to explore, his stomach hopeful for a snack, but he resisted. He doubted he would find anything to eat, anyway.

Surg glanced back at the door, frowning. "Now what?" This wasn't exactly how he'd planned things. His ship was still on that little backwater planet. And no one really knew where he'd gone. He'd told his team he was running down a longshot lead. He hadn't told them where. It hadn't seemed important at the time. What was the worst that could happen?

He frowned. He didn't think Victoria was a bad person, didn't think she would harm him, but intent and results had nothing to do with each other. He'd seen that countless times as a businessman. Actions often had unpredictable consequences. Anymore, though, he didn't "act" much, spending most of his time delegating. It was boring as hell and made him question a lot of the choices he'd made over the years, but that was his life.

Maybe that was why he'd taken such an instant liking to Cass, Kou, and Jessie. Cass and Jessie were irreverent, ignoring his position entirely. And while Kou was certainly deferential at times, he also cared a great deal for the girls, and that said a great deal about the former soldier. He felt like a person around the three. He hadn't felt that way in a long time, not even around his brother.

Surg sighed. None of that mattered at the moment. He didn't have his team or his friends. Just himself. That was all Victoria had as well. Just him. He somehow doubted she would let him reach out to his business, to his team. She was skittish as hell, but he had no idea why. What had spooked her so badly? Why did someone attack her?

He supposed it could have been random, maybe a mugging or just being in the wrong place at the wrong time, but what were the chances of that? In his mind? Slim to none. Something was very wrong, and he needed her to open up if he was going to help her.

Or did he?

She had an onboard AI. Maybe he could get the AI to fill him in. He looked around the room, searching for an interface, but faltered, realizing he didn't know what to call the AI. Most AIs would only respond to their name, so it was important. He wracked his brain, sure he'd heard it at least once before. He remembered her saying a name right before takeoff, but what was it? Was that the AI?

It started with an A sound, but he suspected it was a name from her native tongue, so it had sounded strange to him. It was two syllables, though. "Ang-us?" he said experimentally, sounding out the word carefully.

"Yes?" The AI responded using speakers in the ceiling, the Usan word accented in a way he'd never encountered before.

He turned in surprise, facing the speaker even though the camera was likely elsewhere. "What's going on? What's got Victoria so spooked?"

"I canna say."

"You can't say? I'm here to help."

"Aye, you said that."

Was that suspicion he detected in the simulated voice? He'd never known an AI to be suspicious. That was an emotion. While AIs were quite capable, he used his fair share of them at his company after all, they lacked the ability to make emotional decisions. It made him always hesitant to rely on them too heavily, to put certain things in their control.

Could this AI actually feel emotions? It seemed unlikely, but he could practically *feel* Angus glaring at him, even without a body.

"I *am* here to help. Cass asked me to. You know Cass, right?"

"Yes, Cassandra Allen is the captain of a ship one of my installations is on."

"Yes. She was worried about Victoria."

"You said that already."

"And I meant it."

"We'll see."

CHAPTER FIVE

$\mathcal{V}$ictoria hesitated outside the door to the med bay. *It's just a door. He's just a person.* Somehow, she couldn't convince herself there was nothing to worry about. She didn't have anything specific she *was* worried about with Surg, but the anxiety still ate away at her gut, churning endlessly. It was part of the reason she avoided being around people. She never felt comfortable, always feeling on edge, insecure.

Not to mention, she always walked away feeling drained. She remembered one time when she was making finishing touches on the ship. Her parents had come to visit, had stayed with her. It had been an awkward situation. She'd missed them, missed the old days when things were better. She supposed that was why she'd said okay to them coming by. A part of her must have hoped that they could repair their relationship, that they could move on. She supposed all that chaotic emotion had helped distract her from the claustrophobia that had slowly built, bearing down on her moment after moment. It wasn't until they left that she even noticed it. Afterward, she'd flopped on the floor on her back, feeling like the room was suddenly expansive, like a weight had been lifted.

Yes, Victoria rarely ever wanted to be around people. This was no different. In fact, she'd continued to dawdle, procrastinating by checking the ship again and again, even though she knew she had no choice. She couldn't leave him there, but even so, she'd let herself get distracted.

She continued to stare at the door, her thoughts in chaos. In her exhaustion last night, she'd been in crisis mode, simply unable to think beyond the moment, beyond what was right in front of her, and even that had proven hard. But now? Now, her brain was kicking into gear, her anxiety disorder blending with practical concerns to send her spiraling. What if they'd been followed when they escaped that planet? Her thoughts had been focused on escape, on running, not on evasion. It had never crossed her mind once to wonder if they were being followed. She sighed.

It wouldn't have mattered, anyway. All our monitoring systems are down. I saw to that.

She reminded herself that it was necessary. It made them harder to track, but she now realized it also left them vulnerable, like a blind person with noise canceling headphones on.

Victoria reached for the door to push it open. It unlocked automatically, Angus recognizing her intent. She stepped in, finding Surg standing in the middle of the room, looking pensive. "Come on. I imagine you could use the bathroom."

He turned. "Yes, thank you."

Victoria walked down the central hallway, running her fingers lightly over the smooth metal wall at her side, the sensation easing her a bit. They reached a door, and she pointed. "Through there. There's a bathroom in that room."

She waited in the hall, pressing her back against the cool, hard metal. Her heart pounded erratically, counterpoint to her anxiety. *There's a strange man on my ship. He could be an enemy.* She

37

didn't know what to do. They were stuck together for the unforeseeable future. She could drop him off somewhere, preferably somewhere close-by, but would that be the smart thing? Or, for that matter, would it be fair to him? After all, the universe was enormous, and it would be easy for someone to become stranded. She frowned, feeling guilty even though she hadn't done anything.

I can't abandon him. He saved my life. And she sort of hated herself for that. She hated that she couldn't just dump him somewhere and be done with it. But she wasn't that type of person, even for the sake of her own mental health.

She stared at the open door, trying to think through the problem at hand. She should have come up with a plan before this, but when did she ever remember to plan ahead for social situations? They always seemed to spring surprises on her, ones she couldn't ever anticipate, leaving her stressed and unprepared. So, she had a tendency of thinking she was prepared, then realizing she hadn't prepared well at all.

So what do I do?

She couldn't completely trust him. First, he was a stranger. Second, he could be an enemy. To his advantage, he *had* saved her life, which counted for something, but was it a ruse? She didn't know, and that drove her nuts. He'd said he knew her friend, Cass, but at the moment, she couldn't confirm that.

And so, her thoughts looped around once again, coming back to the core question. Should she operate from a position of him being trustworthy or not? She supposed that, socially, it would be expected that she be grateful for his actions. After all, he *did* get shot because of her. Maybe some hesitant trust was in order. Trust, but verify, as they say.

She let out a sigh, though she couldn't say if it was in relief or not. She'd made her decision to sort of trust him, but that didn't exactly relieve the stress of him being here. If only they could turn the comms back on, she could reach out to Cass and make sure she'd sent him.

That was probably the only thing that eased her about the situation. When he'd told her his connection to Cass, he had to know she could eventually check his story. Hell, for all he knew, she could have turned the comms on the moment after she left him in medical. It would be a risky thing to say if it wasn't true.

The more she thought about it, the more she figured, with a story so easily verifiable, it had to be true, right? He knew Cass. She'd sent him. It certainly sounded like her friend. Well, actually, it would have sounded more like Cass if she had stormed up, loaded to bear and ready for battle. She could easily imagine it, Cass in black tactical gear, guns in both hands, ammo strapped to her body, her little sister trailing behind, but no less lethal. Both of them would rush up to her, and Cass would demand a target to take out.

That she knew of, Cass had never killed a person, human or otherwise, but she didn't doubt the woman would do whatever it took to protect a friend or family member. She was like a momma bear, for all that her sexuality made Victoria uncomfortable most of the time. Cass would do anything for her sister, *had* done everything for her sister. And she'd essentially adopted both Victoria and Ellie, their other friend.

So, she didn't doubt that Cass might send someone to get her, especially if she couldn't find Victoria on her own. And since she'd done so good a job disappearing, it would have been necessary.

A door mechanism clicked, and Surg stepped back out of the room moments later, closing the door behind him.

The room he'd just left was the only other bedroom besides her own. It usually remained empty, probably collecting dust at an alarming rate as guests just didn't stay overnight on her ship. In fact, now that she thought about it, she wondered why she even *had* a guest room. Why did she do it? Was it some errant hope for a social life she would never have? She didn't know, and she shrugged the thoughts off. "You can stay in there while you're here."

He looked behind him at the blank door, then turned back to face her. "Does that mean you trust me now?"

"I'm giving you a shot. Don't screw it up," she said, trying to channel Cass. Even to herself, it didn't sound convincing.

"Of course."

"Come on. Let's get something to eat." She always did a bit better socially when she was multitasking. Or at least, she didn't feel as stressed about it. Then her stomach growled, reminding her that she hadn't eaten since early yesterday. She picked up the pace.

The galley was just down the hall, a narrow space with a refrigerator, robotic cooking station, and lots of cupboards. "What do you want?" she asked as she approached the robot's control panel.

"Something quick is fine."

She nodded, picking a couple sandwiches and teas. The robot whirred to life, pulling out ingredients from the side opening of the fridge. She kept her back facing Surg, procrastinating the moment she would actually have to deal with him. It was cowardly, but what else was new?

A couple minutes later, the robot spat out sandwiches on two plates along with two distinctly different tea cups. One was cream with dainty pink flowers, while the other had a picture of an anime character on it. She passed half the items over to Surg and leaned against the counter, setting her own plate and cup aside to eat with both hands. She chewed thoughtfully, trying to figure out what to say. The bread was soft, almost mushy, while crisp lettuce crunched in her mouth. She didn't usually add lettuce to her sandwiches, but she hadn't been thinking, hadn't remembered to customize the system's default. Good thing the turkey club she'd picked didn't include anything nasty.

Victoria swallowed, looking over at Surg, who wasn't quite as absorbed in his sandwich as she had been. He was watching her.

What's he thinking?

Didn't matter. But they did have some things to discuss. She had half a thought of trying to catch him in a lie, but she doubted she could pull it off. Still, trying to verify his story a bit wouldn't hurt. "So, you know about the call with Cass. What did she tell you?"

He finished his bite before speaking. "Said the comm was compromised, that afterward she couldn't get in touch with you. Even the tracker she'd put on your ship wasn't sending a signal."

Victoria had put her sandwich down and nodded along, slowly sipping her tea now. The warmth of the cup was soothing and her finger idly ran over the raised flower design. "Wait, what?" she said, spraying hot tea across the floor and the front panel of the cooking robot as his words sank in. "Crap." She put down her cup, shaking her hands and wiping them off where they'd received some of the spray.

"Towels?"

"That cabinet," she said, pointing across the room.

He nodded and pulled out a cloth towel before moving over and wiping down the robot, then the floor, then dropping the damp cloth on the counter. "That was a bit of a reaction," he said, a small smile on his face.

"Cass had a tracker on me?" She was simultaneously surprised, dismayed, and resigned. Of *course*, Cass had a tracker on her. This was Cass, after all. The ultimate mother hen.

"Yes, although I guess it didn't occur to me that she didn't tell you. Anyway, can you tell me more about what happened?"

Victoria paused, wondering how much she should trust him. What should she tell him? What was safe? "Well, not knowing what was going on, and considering I'd *just* had a break-through in my research, I was cautious. I shut down comms. Unfortunately, we weren't able to trace the bug. I can't tell if it's hardware or software. I don't know if anything else is compromised. In the end, after some hefty investigating, I decided to shut down *everything* that could send an outside signal. That seemed safest under the circumstances."

He swallowed, and she watched his throat bob with the action. "I noticed. That's actually how I found you on that planet."

"What?!" Her hands jerked as she pushed up off the counter, but this time she didn't spill.

He shrugged. "Not a lot of ships run without any signals. It tends to get noticed if there's a discrepancy like that. If you've got the right connections, you can track that type of information."

"Great," she said. Turning around, she dropped her cup next to her plate and pressed her hands against the counter's edge, feeling defeated. "I'm pitiful." She shook her head.

"You're not pitiful."

She felt him approaching behind her and tensed.

"You managed to keep yourself pretty well hidden."

She scoffed, turning around to face him. He'd backed up, giving her space again. "Hidden? Both you *and* my attacker found me. Not exactly hiding well, was I?"

He smirked. "No matter how good you are, there's usually someone better. And playing offense is a lot easier than defense."

"What do you mean?"

"Well, look at security. A security team and security system have to block out every avenue of entrance. But an intruder only needs to find one gap. Finding a single gap is a lot easier."

"Makes sense."

"So, we need to find out what they've done to the ship, and who did it."

Victoria shook her head. "I've been trying. I feel like I've torn this ship apart trying. Whatever they did wiped all evidence of not only where they sent the information, but where it originated. It can't be found."

Surg leaned back against the refrigerator, plate still held in one hand. "Maybe it can."

"How?" She threw her hands up, waving them a couple times before stopping herself.

"I assume you've been looking for the coding."

"Of course. But do you have any idea how many lines of code there are on this ship? Add to that, Angus is a learning computer. That means he adds lines of code that didn't originally exist. He can do a lot, but he hasn't had any luck with finding something out of place."

"Maybe I can help with the search. Outside perspective you know? I don't know anything about human programming language, but I've seen my fair share of other programming languages. Most likely, the coding will be of non-human origin. And if we can figure out which one, it will tell us something about your programmer."

"Like what? It's just a programming language."

"True, but there are a lot of species out there. People often use programming languages in line with their native tongue, their native species."

She leaned forward, getting excited. "So, if we can figure out which language was used, we might be able to narrow down the culprits." She became giddy for a moment, but then deflated. "What is that gonna matter? Narrowing down suspects doesn't help when we don't *have* any suspects."

"Well, you said yourself. It happened immediately after you had a breakthrough. If we know what the breakthrough is, and we can narrow down by species or language, we've got somewhere to start. I mean, how many people do you think would be interested in this discovery, interested enough to spy on you and attack you?"

She shook her head. "I have no idea. But if someone were going to exploit it, they would need resources. Big company. Probably a design or manufacturing company related to transportation or spaceship construction and parts."

"Why is that?"

"Because I think I discovered a means of instantaneous transportation."

CHAPTER SIX

*S*urg sat in the cockpit. The space was stark and cramped, with displays and controls all around him. The seat was fairly comfortable, but not after so many hours sitting in it. By now, his back was starting to hurt. This chair was *not* designed with his spine in mind.

He was starting to regret offering to help. It had been a long, drawn-out process. First, he'd needed to learn the basics of human coding, then he'd worked with Angus to find key variants between the coding the ship was designed on and what other species would use.

It was disheartening as he considered how many different programming languages there truly were. And while it turned out Angus *could* look up programming languages using database searches, he couldn't do that while offline. He was flying blind, just the same as the rest of them.

Somehow, he suspected the AI would be researching programming languages in depth once he was back online…

But for now, they'd gotten into a pattern, with Surg setting up search parameters for each language while Angus hunted for elements from the previous ones.

He still couldn't believe Victoria had invented a means of instantaneous travel. The very concept of it was mind-boggling, revolutionary. The mercenary businessman in him immediately thought of the financial potential of such a discovery, but he squashed it. There were more important things to think about.

Like who would benefit from such a technology.

Unfortunately, the list was long, ranging from planetary governments and criminals to large businesses like his own. Personally, he would never resort to such practices, but he wouldn't put it past some of his competitors, like the Diehli. He'd crossed swords with them many a time in the past, and he knew what they were like. In fact, that was how he'd met Victoria's friend, Cass. She'd inadvertently gotten between his company and the animals at Diehli, and it could have gotten her killed. The Diehli guys were ruthless, willing to go to great lengths to get what they wanted.

Could they be behind this?

It was possible, but he had to remind himself it was just one of many possibilities out there. And theorizing about them wasn't going to solve the problem at hand. After all, why borrow trouble when they already had trouble to spare?

"I found something," Angus said over the intercom hours later.

Surg looked up, then behind him at the stark, empty hallway leading to the rest of the ship. "Is Victoria coming here?"

"Yes."

He nodded. "Good." His curiosity teased his brain, but he kept still, accustomed to waiting. In his life, it had been a virtue, sometimes cultivated, sometimes thrust upon him, but often necessary for success and survival.

He perked up when Victoria suddenly appeared, jogging down the hall, her soft footsteps lightly clapping against the floor tiles. The sound was quiet, too quiet, and he wondered what type of shoes she was wearing. He'd honestly heard infiltration specialists that made more noise while running.

"What did you find?" she said, out of breath. She shook out her hands and straightened.

"There was a hidden subroutine in the communications controller. I'm still looking for other code."

Victoria bobbed on her feet. "That means we can bypass it and send comms unnoticed, right?"

"Yes," Angus said. "I can either reprogram the comms to avoid the subroutine, which will take time, or I can just remove it entirely."

"Remove," Victoria said instantly.

But Surg had another idea. "Bypass it."

"What?!" she turned on him, looking shocked. "Why would we keep it?"

He leaned closer. "They clearly know about you, know about your research. If we just delete the subroutine right away, then you'll always be under threat by them."

She blanched, her hands vibrating at her sides. "This won't end?" Her voice was quiet, frail.

He shook his head, his hair brushing against his cheeks, teasing the edges of his peripheral vision. "No, not unless we stop them."

She sagged against the nearest surface, the far left edge of the control system. "Then what do we do?"

"Well, we need to first find everything they've changed on your ship." Not an easy task, and they didn't have access to the resources he normally would. He was tempted to call in the team he'd organized to find Victoria, but he couldn't, not until he could send a secure comm. "Then we need to figure out who is behind this and why."

She scoffed. "The *why* is easy. Profit. Power. You name it."

"Those are two reasons and knowing the motives can narrow down the suspects. Listen, I've got a lot of connections. I can try to put a list together of organizations that might be behind this."

"You can?"

"Yeah. But in the end, that's just conjecture. I would say the *best* way to figure out who's behind this is a trap."

"A trap?" Her voice went thin again.

He nodded. "Yup. We lure them in, capture them, and get them to talk. Unless they hired professional mercenaries through intermediaries, which is actually pretty unlikely, the people after you *know* who's behind it."

"Why do you say that's unlikely?"

"Well, first, you've been avoiding them for weeks. No mercenary team would wait that long to strike. After all, it would only take boarding your ship to complete their job."

"Maybe they'd hoped to get the information with no one the wiser."

"I doubt it. This is too slow. If they'd truly wanted to keep things quiet, they already failed. There're too many people involved, too many people to point fingers at them. If you want to keep things quiet, you act decisively. Just a single strike is all it takes. No witnesses. No survivors."

"Who would do that?"

He shrugged. "A lot of large companies set up shop outside of regulated zones for that very reason. Stay out of a government's jurisdiction, and you can do whatever you want with no one to stop you." He shook his head. "It's amazing what people will do when they know they won't get caught."

"Jesus."

He frowned. He didn't recognize the word, but it sounded like some sort of exclamation, so he moved on, leaning forward over the arm rest. "If one of those companies is behind this, they'll stop at *nothing* to get what they want."

CHAPTER SEVEN

*A*ngus had finished his scan of the computer systems. He'd found one other subroutine in their navigation system. It was connected to a burst transmitter, which meant someone had been on her ship. She shivered at the idea, feeling slightly violated. But once she pushed beyond that, the question became, how the hell did they get on the *Discovery*? She was careful, maybe even a little paranoid. It should have been impossible, right?

Victoria reached her hand into the open panel below the control dashboard. She had a flashlight clipped to her sleeve, illuminating the maze of wires and circuit boards underneath the console. She spotted the transmitter immediately and pulled it toward her. With her other hand, she reached behind her for a tool.

She needed to add a regulator so it could only send signals when *she* wanted it to. It was pretty easy, really. She'd gone to her lab and wired up a remote control switch. Then she'd given Angus control of the switch so he could send a signal when they wanted to spring the trap.

Her fingers ran over the coarse wire and smooth outer coating. She'd put on her noise canceling headphones and some nice instrumental rock music so she could focus. Ships were noisy places, and she'd always functioned better when she didn't have distractions.

"Done," she said to no one, pulling back and dropping her tool in the bag next to her.

Now all they needed to do was turn comms back on. Her gut churned at the idea, remembering that terrifying moment when Angus had interrupted her call with Cass. What if they'd screwed it up? What if they'd missed something? The whole plan relied on them finding all the bugs. If they missed something, the people after her would get conflicting information and would know something was up.

She reached for the screwdriver, gripping the tool's handle hard. The plastic creaked in her fist. She grabbed the panel to her right and lined it up, securing it one screw at a time. With the plan in motion, her thoughts drifted to other things, like her research.

It was never far from her mind, and not just because it was at the center of this whole mess. Her research was her sanctuary. When she couldn't deal with the world, she retreated into it, burying her head in her work until everything else went away, until it didn't matter anymore. She wished she could say it was just a passion for the science, but she knew better. Deep down, she had to admit she'd used it far too many times to hide from realities she couldn't cope with.

Now all her research was secured away and encrypted to hell and back. She was the only person who could decrypt it. Not even Angus could break the encryptions. She'd seen to that. Only she knew the decryption code and it couldn't be hacked, couldn't be broken, not without forcing a wipe. It also couldn't be copied, not until she entered the code.

Her data was safe.

If only she could say the same for herself.

Victoria sat in her seat in the cockpit, anxiety buzzing through her. It had been weeks since she'd talked to anyone but Angus and now Surg. She took a deep breath as she prepared herself to make the call. She'd always found it harder to interact with people after a bout of isolation. This time was no different.

"Call Cass," she said, biting the bullet as her stomach churned with anxiety.

"Calling."

She rubbed her middle and index fingers against each other in repetitive circles, letting the gentle pattern soothe her as she waited for the call to connect.

"What the fuck, Vicky?" Cass exploded as the call finally connected. "Where the hell have you been?" Cass's entire body was alive with her outrage, practically screaming it through the video call.

Victoria looked away, feeling guilty about her absence. "Sorry," she finally said sheepishly.

Cass sighed, and Victoria looked up. Cass was just staring at the camera, her messy bedroom in the background.

"What is it?" Victoria said.

"You had us all worried. Are you okay?"

"I will be," she said, trying to sound more confident than she felt.

"What does that mean?" Cass leaned forward, her body tensing.

"I could use your help, Cass."

"Anything. You know that."

"Thanks." Except now she didn't know where to start. What could she say? Should she start with what she needed from Cass? Should she start by apologizing? Wait… did she already apologize? She wracked her brain, but couldn't recall.

It didn't matter. She took a deep breath, deciding to start at the beginning. "So, about our last call…"

"We are in place," Angus said over the intercom. "Waiting for Cass to report in."

Surg looked up from his position seated on his bed. The room was clearly an afterthought. He was honestly surprised it had bedding in it, since it looked like no one had ever entered it before.

It had a bed and bedside table with a layer of dust on it and nothing else. He readjusted his sleeves as he stepped out into the hallway. The halls were empty, and he turned left toward the cockpit. He supposed he could have gone anywhere. He really had nothing to do at this point but wait. And if he was going to wait, he figured he might as well keep Victoria company.

After they'd found the bugs and isolated them, Victoria had contacted Cass, and they'd come up with a plan. Between Surg, Cass, and Angus, they'd found a location where Cass's ship, the *Trojan*, could remain out of sight while leaving the *Discovery* appearing isolated and "hidden." They wanted their pursuers to feel safe, like she was ripe for the picking, but also like Victoria didn't realize just how vulnerable she truly was.

After all, a good trap left the prey feeling like *they* were doing the hunting.

As he reached the cockpit, it was empty. He turned, wondering where else Victoria might have gone. The kitchen and lab seemed the most likely. She didn't seem to spend a lot of time in her room, and he got the impression she preferred being busy.

He fled the cockpit and passed the kitchen. Only a momentary glance told him she wasn't there either.

The lab it was, then. The lab was at the far back of the ship, in the area most ships held cargo and supplies. He'd been on the ship long enough to know she did keep some supplies back there, but most of the area was a dedicated workspace.

He crossed into the large room, spotting her at a countertop to the left, the soft sound of her voice reaching him, absent of words. The room was dwarfed by equipment lining the opposite wall, most of which he could only guess at the purpose of. "Hey, Victoria."

She looked up, but seemed a little lost.

"Are you okay?" He approached, cautious as she continued to look around her, seeming disconnected, detached.

"I guess. I don't like waiting."

He laughed, drawing her attention. She tilted her head slightly, reminding him of the standard greeting for his people. "Nobody likes waiting." The space didn't seem to have another chair, so he popped a squat on a tall box and pulled it up beside her. The edges dug into his thighs, but he ignored it.

She started rubbing her hands on her pants legs. He watched as she continued. He'd seen plenty of people commit that motion, but usually just to clean them or dry them. Victoria, conversely, kept doing it long after her hands should be dry. Was it some sort of nervous tick?

"Hey," he said, running his hands lightly over the backs of hers, but not trying to hold them or stop them. "It's gonna be fine. It's gonna be a long wait, but everything's gonna work out."

She shook her head. "You don't know that."

He smirked. "I don't know… I think I do. I'm not someone used to failure. And failure is giving up. After all, everyone stumbles."

"I know," she said, but his words didn't seem to make any difference. Her hands continued to work her pants again and again.

"Well," he said, standing from his box. "There's no point sitting around waiting for Cass to show up." He rubbed his hands together. "What can we do to be productive in the meantime?"

She finally stopped, her thumb running thoughtfully back and forth as she stared off into the distance. "I guess we could put a few things back together."

"Back together?"

She smiled. "Yeah. When I was trying to find the bugs, I kind of dismantled a lot of things." She looked away, her hands resuming their pattern on her thighs.

"Right." He reached out to her. "Well, then, let's get to work."

She looked back up at him, her smile resuming as her hands dropped to her sides. "Yes, let's."

Surg yawned, enjoying the manual labor for once. Sure, he was feeling the effects after hours of this, but it felt nostalgic. His hands hurt from clenching tools in his fists, he had a cut on his finger from a metal panel he'd replaced in the maintenance corridor, and his knees felt like they'd been ground to pulp from kneeling on the floor. But each sensation made him smile, reminding him of when he'd first started his company. Back then, it was just him, and he'd been forced to wear a lot of hats. Eventually, he'd pulled his brother into the business, and they'd worked side by side, building a better future for themselves. He missed those days. Nowadays, he rarely ever saw his brother.

When had they become so distant?

When had success become more important than the people in his life?

He didn't know, but he was really enjoying his time here with Victoria. She was an interesting person, a puzzle he would love to solve. As they put everything to rights, he'd asked her about her work, which had resulted in a deluge of information, most of which he couldn't hope to understand. He got little glimpses, little ideas, but most of it went right over his head.

Regardless, the passion with which she talked, the pure joy on her face when she enthused about it, was enchanting. He wanted to ask her questions just to see that expression once more. When was the last time he'd been around someone with so much energy? Sometimes, when she talked, she got so excited, she couldn't sit still, her arms, hands, her entire body alive with motion. Had he ever felt that way himself?

Surg remembered desperation and pain. He remembered determination. He remembered the drive to protect his little brother, to provide for him, to make sure he wanted for nothing ever again. But had he ever felt about *anything* the way she did about her research? He didn't think so.

She turned back, her face lighting up as she made a point.

Damn, but she was beautiful like that.

CHAPTER EIGHT

*V*ictoria sat in her lab staring off into space, the shapes blurring into an abstract painting. Around her, the ship hummed, the sound vibrating through her. They were nearly done with their preparations and had taken a dinner break. Surg was eating in his room, giving her space.

It wasn't the first time he'd done something like that, though, and she couldn't get it out of her head. Extended periods of time around other people always followed specific patterns. She would either insult them accidentally or their eyes would glaze over when she started talking about her work. Hell, she'd even overwhelmed people in her field, people who'd gone to school for it. She would see that look in their eyes, that moment of "I have no idea what she's talking about," and die a little inside. It was very isolating.

Hell, if it wasn't for Cass taking her under her wing, she wouldn't even have the few friends she *did* have. Cass had seen her as a lost kitten or something, in need of a home. As such, no matter what Victoria did to screw things up, Cass just kept coming back for more. Victoria would insult her, and Cass would laugh it off. Victoria would drone on about her work, and Cass would chime in with her own work or change the subject. Cass was the first person to not treat her like a total weirdo.

And yet, even her relationship with Cass wasn't as easy as her relationship with Surg. She rarely *chose* to spend time with Cass. Her friend almost always initiated, and sometimes Victoria wasn't exactly appreciative of those efforts. It was jarring to have someone foist themselves into your space like that.

Cass also tried to force certain expectations on Victoria, like communication. Sure, Cass was better than most, often giving her space when she needed it, but it wasn't always the *right* amount of space, and she rarely recognized when she pushed Victoria too far.

It was different with Surg, though. It was easier. The first thing she'd noticed was how he often backed away, sometimes physically, when she needed it. He didn't push her too far, even when he probably should have.

And while they'd been working, he didn't seem to mind when she slipped into talking about her research. Victoria had gone on and on for hours, but he never tried to change the subject, nor did he treat her like she was weird. She'd never had that before.

She kind of liked it.

I'm hopeless.

As they finished up for the day, Surg couldn't help himself. There was just something about her, something captivating, energizing. They'd been talking and working all day, and the contrast between working with her and his life before her was stark.

I don't want to go back.

It was a little startling. He had an enormous business, was rich, was influential, powerful even, but he didn't want to go back. He didn't want to go back to his empty, tastefully decorated rooms, his brother he never saw, and his job that no longer piqued his interest.

Surg remembered when he was growing the business, it had been interesting, exciting. He'd felt driven, energized to start each day, ready to conquer mountains.

When had that stopped?

And at what point had doing a favor for a business associate become something more? Yes, he found Victoria fascinating, stunning even when she was passionate about something, but so what? It wasn't like she was his partner...

No...

Could she be, though? Except he didn't remember feeling attracted to her from the start. Wasn't that the first identifier? Then again, he'd been injured. Could an injury make it harder to detect? Partners were a biologically driven instinct for his kind. You were supposed to just *know*. He supposed, in the grand scheme of things, it didn't matter.

For years, he'd been a bit uncertain of how he felt about biological partners. When he was younger, he'd seen it as a cage. He hadn't wanted a partner, hadn't wanted to have choice taken away from him. He'd been certain that building his business and providing for his brother were the epitome of life for him. When he'd looked at those biology-driven relationships, he'd noticed only the failures, the ones who never developed affection or even hated each other.

But as time passed, and his business grew more successful, both the business and Varn needing him less, he'd realized his life didn't seem complete. Surg had received everything he'd ever wanted, and yet it wasn't what he needed. He'd started looking to the partners around him, seeing the successful pairings for possibly the first time. He'd started fantasizing about finding one himself, but he spent so little time with members of his own species, and there had never been a single biological pairing between members of different species.

Hope had begun to feel like a heavy weight bearing down on him, and the idea of a companion in his life, a partner of any sort, even a mundane one, seemed completely out of reach. There were times when the loneliness had been a bit too much, overwhelming him in weak moments. He'd laughed it off, played matchmaker from time to time, pried into other people's relationships, but more than anything, he'd just wanted someone of his own.

"Okay, that's it," Victoria said, rubbing her hands together before starting to put her tools back in the bag.

"Great." Except he didn't want the day to end. Somehow, at some point, she'd become more than just someone he'd offered to help. But how much more?

He followed her out of a dim maintenance corridor, stepping out into her lab. The sudden change in light whited out his vision, and he blinked, his hand automatically reaching to shade his eyes.

Victoria dropped her tools on a countertop and walked away toward the hallway. Surg followed her without thinking. It seemed automatic by now, like the actions of a trained pet.

The day was over. They were probably both tired, ready for their beds.

And yet, Surg didn't want to sleep. Victoria stopped to open her door, and his mouth opened. "Victoria?"

"Yes?" She turned around and looked up at him.

He hadn't really noticed how short she was until that very moment. He leaned down and kissed her, the clothes on his back pulling as he bent down. But once their lips met, his clothing was the last thing on his mind. Her lips were soft, just barely parted, and frozen in place, like she didn't know what to do with them. Her breath puffed out as he pulled away.

"Good night."

He stood there, dumbfounded.

This moment felt like an epiphany, like his world had been off its axis and had suddenly returned to its proper alignment. He sighed as she closed the door.

To the void with partners, he thought with a smile. He would follow her anywhere.

Victoria touched her lips, shocked by the kiss. She listened, back pressed to the other side of her door as Surg turned and walked away, the door to his own room clicking closed a moment later.

He kissed me.

She hadn't expected that. It hadn't even popped up on her radar. Then again, she'd never been good at romance. After all, how many times had she accidentally flirted with someone or found herself suddenly in an uncomfortable situation because she couldn't tell when someone was hitting on her?

After an indeterminate time, she shook herself out of her stupor. The doorknob was poking into her lower back so she stepped away from the door to alleviate the discomfort. Around her, everything felt a little different, like it wasn't *her* room, *her* ship.

She continued to run her fingertips lightly back and forth over her lips, feeling every crack and dry spot. The kiss had been different. She'd been kissed before, but never by an alien. His different facial structure had been interesting, making her suddenly curious to explore it in more detail. She wanted to run her fingers over his lips, his skin, his nose. Did he have stubble, or would he be smooth?

What made that kiss so much different? Sure, he was an alien, but that couldn't be it. She'd never been interested in aliens, really. Mostly, she didn't notice anyone, so what made him so different? Why did she notice *him*? She should be furious with him. He hadn't asked. He'd just leaned in and kissed her. Shouldn't she be upset about that?

But she wasn't. Sure, her stomach was churning furiously, but she knew herself. She always got anxious when she was dealing with the unknown, and she'd never been in this position before.

She actually *wanted* to kiss him again.

———

Victoria woke up and stretched, her soft sheets sliding over her barely clad skin. The bedding was perfect, and the result of a great deal of hunting, as she was rather picky. It was hard finding material that felt soft, but didn't make noise when she tossed and turned. The noise would keep her from falling asleep.

She sighed, for once reveling in a feeling of contentment and comfort first thing in the morning. Unfortunately, that didn't last long, and soon, her mind was back to its normal, overactive self.

And the first topic at hand? Last night's kiss.

I didn't even tell him good night.

"Stupid," she shook her head and sat up. "Angus, what's our status?"

"Cass arrived overnight and is in place on the dark side of the asteroid, as planned. The magnetic properties of the rock should adversely affect sensor systems."

She stood up, reaching for something to wear. "Can you sense her ship?"

"Barely, but only because I'm specifically looking. I know the exact specs of the ship, so finding it is easier. Our pursuers will have no reason to check so thoroughly, or with that degree of specificity."

She nodded as she pulled a shirt over her head. "Right." Somehow, she managed to absently don pants, socks, and shoes before opening her bedroom door and wandering to the galley.

"Nice combo," Surg said as she entered. He had a cup of something hot in front of him as he sat on the counter.

Victoria looked down and groaned. She'd managed to put on the only clothing in her entire repertoire that didn't match. Usually, she picked jeans or black pants so she didn't have to pay attention to what she wore. It was an old habit from working in corporate America, where appearances actually mattered.

These pants, on the other hand, were a lime green that almost hurt the eyes. They'd been cheap and really comfortable. The moment she'd touched the material, she hadn't been able to let it go. And when she'd tried them on and they fit like a glove, she'd had no excuse not to buy them. Unfortunately, they clashed horribly with her tee shirt today. It was chocolate brown with a picture of a squirrel on it and letters underneath that read, "Protect your nuts."

She shrugged. Honestly, for all she knew, she could have made this combination countless times before and not even realized.

Victoria walked to the control panel and picked something to eat.

Behind her, Surg laughed.

She turned, expecting him to be making fun of her, but she didn't feel the normal animosity she did when people laughed around her. She didn't feel the uncertainty. Surg was relaxed and had returned his focus back to his beverage. She didn't know what to think, so she pushed it out of her mind, returning to the robot to collect her meal as the bowl clattered onto the deck.

Victoria pushed the noodles around, not sure what to do with herself. She didn't want to leave the room, but didn't like eating while standing. She thought about sitting on the counter, but the room was tiny and she would be forced to sit right next to him, which she wasn't quite comfortable doing. The floor was a similar problem. Sitting there would have him looming over her.

He looked up from his cup. "Hm. This room isn't exactly ideal for eating, is it?"

"No. But then, it's not a dining room. This ship was designed for a small crew, optimally two. It can handle more if necessary, but the ship wasn't really designed for it. I just needed to create a ship that could handle the natural variations that you might experience, including guests and periods of heightened oxygen consumption."

"Like exercise, fear, things like that?"

Victoria snorted. "And sex."

Surg coughed. "What?"

"What, you've met Cass. I've barely had a single conversation with her that didn't either revolve back to sex or have some sort of sexual innuendo in it. It's like it's all she thinks about."

"I hadn't noticed."

She sighed and put down her fork. "Well, she has calmed down a bit since finding Kou. She's been different. I'm thinking in a good way, though it's too soon to tell."

"Yeah." He put down his own cup on the counter beside him. "I think she's good for him, too." He smirked. "You know, I kind of nudged them together."

She laughed. "You did?"

"Oh, yeah. They were a mess."

"Why am I not surprised?"

"Ahem," Angus interrupted.

"Yes, Angus?"

"Would you like me to send out the ping?"

Right, the trap. The plan was to send a ping of their location to the people out to get her, drawing them into their clutches. Since the ping would be coming from the equipment the bad guys had planted on her ship, it should pull them right in without being the wiser.

"Yes, Angus. Go for it."

"And now, we wait," Surg said, picking up his cup once more.

Yes, now we wait.

Surg couldn't stop thinking about that kiss.

Why the hell did I do that?

He looked over at her, trying to decipher her mood. She danced about the kitchen with swift, easy movements. Before long, she handed him a meal, and he stared down at it. He didn't recognize it. There were a variety of colors and shapes, but it meant nothing to him. He chewed slowly, the foods at times savory, sweet, or spicy, but he didn't pay much attention to them.

Instead, he returned his focus to *her*. Did he push her too far? It was hard to tell. He tried to watch her covertly, but it wasn't always easy to read her. Utensils clacked against dishes, and occasionally, he could hear her sipping her tea. She seemed fine, seemed to be handling it okay, but what if he was wrong? What if she was trying to avoid a repeat performance without making it weird? After all, they were stuck on this ship together. She was relying on his help to stop these guys. Could she really afford to alienate him?

Man, I really screwed this up.

He returned his focus to his plate, pushing his pointed utensil through the various foods until they started to blend together. This was so strange. He felt all out of sorts. Usually, he was this person of authority, someone people sought out for direction, and yet he needed direction more than anyone right now. He was screwing everything up, and he didn't have a clue how to fix it.

But, then again, what was he screwing up?

That thought gave him pause. He'd made a promise to Cass, one he'd already upheld by just searching for Victoria. Staying with her, helping her set a trap, these were both above and beyond the call of duty. He didn't need to do this.

But I want to.

But why? What was drawing him here? Why was he so enamored with her? Why did this matter so much to him? He didn't know, and he wasn't overly inclined to explore those questions at the moment.

So, instead, he moved to wash his dishes, deciding a little manual labor would get him out of his head, but Victoria halted him with a hand on his arm.

He froze.

"I've got this."

He looked down at her. "It's all right." He shrugged. "There's not much else I can help with at the moment. And I'm sure you have better things you could be doing. I mean, this is *your* ship."

She shrugged, her body a breath away from him. "We're just waiting at this point. What else am I going to do?"

He searched her face, her body language, but didn't know, couldn't tell. Was she okay? Did his stupidity ruin this thing they had between them?

CHAPTER NINE

I'm useless at this.

Victoria had wanted to hold on and never let go when she'd touched his forearm, the tight muscles there fascinating her. But he'd immediately tensed, his body language screaming discomfort. So she'd let go, feeling like she'd done something wrong.

He started washing dishes as she stood there, the space between them filling with silence. She wasn't good at initiating, but it was clear he wasn't going to discuss the elephant in the room, the kiss.

It was all she could think about, though.

She wanted to talk about it. She wanted to explore this further, but she also suspected she would need to make the next move. Surge was just too good at giving her the space she needed, and this wasn't the time for it. She wanted to immerse herself in whatever they had between them.

And there was no time like the present because they were currently waiting for the people who'd spied on her, who'd attacked her, to show up. All they could do now was wait.

She smirked. Except maybe explore each other. She watched him while his back was turned, her fingers running over her lip as she remembered the kiss. His shirt looked thin and soft, lightly outlining his muscles in teasing glimpses as he worked his hands in the soapy water. Looking at him was easier this way, with his back turned. She didn't have to look him in the eyes, in the face. The pressure seemed lower. She felt like she could do anything, say anything.

What am I thinking? I can't do this.

She was better at relating to her research than actual people. What if she screwed this up? She didn't want him to look poorly on her like so many people had in the past. Or dismiss her like almost everyone else did.

Stop it.

It was hard, reminding herself not to spiral into anxiety and worst-case scenarios. It was so easy to imagine all the ways it could go wrong. But nothing was guaranteed in life. She knew that. She'd *experienced* that. People she should have been able to rely on had betrayed her, used her.

But just because something wasn't permanent, didn't mean it wasn't worthwhile. They could fool around, enjoy one another, right? Even if it never amounted to anything, it could still be fond memories, right?

Surg felt like he was walking on ice, like the slightest misstep would cause it to crack under his weight. He was trying to keep it casual, trying not to push her. She didn't *seem* to be showing any signs of distress, but she was another species. Could he be missing something? Could he *really* rely on his experiences to read her?

The day was nearly over. Things had been strained, but they'd spent a significant part of the day playing a role playing game with Angus, which had distracted him from the tension in the air.

The game was like nothing he'd ever encountered. It seemed to involve a lot of chance and combat, battling monsters unlike anything he'd imagined in his life. Were they actual creatures from her planet or make believe?

Like the day before, he followed her as they moved to their respective bedrooms at the end of the day. Nerves gnawed at him, and his indecision grew. Should he just say good night? Should he kiss her again? Would she even be amenable to that?

Why had he kissed her in the first place? It had been an impulse, not thought through at all, and it wasn't like him. He hadn't acted like that since he was a near-adult still struggling to understanding his sexuality.

He stopped next to her as she reached her door. She turned around to face him, a small smile gracing her face. She looked slightly sleepy, her body relaxed as she stood there watching him.

He opened his mouth to tell her good night, but Victoria shook her head. "Bend over a bit."

He frowned, but did as she requested, wondering what she was up to.

"You are just too damn tall," she said, then grabbed his shirt and pulled him in for a kiss.

Finally.

Victoria leaned hard into the kiss, enjoying the moment, wanting it to last forever. She gripped his shirt, holding on for dear life. The fabric bunched in her hand, digging into her fingers.

When she pulled away, her entire body was tense, waiting for his reaction. She couldn't look him in the eye, instead rubbing her fingers across the shirt material in front of her.

What have I done?

Then a finger pressed under her chin, lifting up her face. For a brief moment, she saw the intention in his eyes, then he dived in, devouring her lips. Their previous kisses were a pale comparison to this one. She couldn't breathe, wanted to spiral in all directions at once. She *needed*, but her brain was too muddled to say *what*.

Victoria whimpered, then the door at her back gave, and they tumbled into the room. Skin touched skin, hands exploring mindlessly, like they were magnets attracted to opposite poles.

Her fingers brushed the waistband of his pants as the backs of her legs bumped into the bed. She fell, her digits reflexively digging under the coarse material at her fingertips, drawing him down on top of her.

He came down hard, and she yelped.

"Sorry," he said, pushing up off her. "You are so beautiful."

She frowned. "No, I'm not."

He looked at her, incredulous, and ran a hand through her hair. "Well, maybe you're my kind of beautiful."

She laughed, but he was serious. "Really?"

He nodded. "Really."

Her hand curled deeper under his waistband, pulling him tighter against her. "We need to be wearing less clothing."

He smirked. "Really? This is too much?"

She smacked his shoulder. "Don't kill the moment."

He grew serious in a snap. "Oh, I wouldn't dream of it." His head dipped down, taking her lips once more.

She leaned in, her chest rubbing against his as she fiddled with his pants.

"Impatient," he said, whispering into her ear as his hands wandered up, pushing her shirt out of the way.

"Oh, I can be when I'm properly motivated." She almost held her breath as his touch continued north, the cooler air of the ship's atmospherics sending goosebumps across her exposed skin.

Victoria tilted her head to the side as Surg moved his lips to her neck. Her eyes lolled about as he made contact, her gaze dropping down and stopping at the pants he shouldn't be wearing. "Surg, if you don't take your pants off, I'm *going* to shred them." She was a shape-shifter, and while she rarely used the abilities overtly, the more Surg touched and kissed her, the more she wanted, needed. She could easily form claws and just rip his pants from his body. And with her own body strung tight, her breath quickening, and her blunt nails digging into his arms as he continued his ministrations, claws were seeming an increasingly good idea. "And it's not like you have a spare," she continued, her voice breathy as she struggled for sanity.

He laughed and pulled back, his knees causing the bed to dip under his weight. She frowned at him as he moved away, her mind and body completely at odds.

"Couldn't have that, now could we?" He smirked. "Although... wandering the ship naked would be quite a distraction for our trap.

"Don't even think about it."

It took a flick of a finger for him to unfasten his pants, exposing a V of skin.

"Then again, the view's not bad." She smiled, reaching for him again.

"Shirts," he said as he pulled his own over his head.

She nodded, following his example. She lost sight of him for a moment, but then their hands were on each other again, and newly exposed skin touched. Victoria explored as she kicked at her pants, trying to get rid of them.

Surg leaned in next to her ear once more, his breath hot against her neck. "Shoes, Vic."

She growled, getting more frantic as he laughed at her.

"You really are impatient."

She glared at him. "Fix it."

"Yes, ma'am." He pulled back for hopefully the last time and pulled her shoes off. Then he grabbed the ankles of her pants and pulled again, nearly dragging her off the bed.

She laughed as her ass settled over mid air.

He dropped overtop her.

"You know, I'm still wearing panties, right?"

He looked down between them and then back into her eyes. "Huh. I better do something about that." Putting his hands on the fabric at her hips, he dropped his lips to her shoulder. His hands and mouth worked in concert, and she tensed. He moved farther and farther down, moving out of her reach. She felt nothing but his lips and the gentle slide of fabric shifting down her legs. She gripped the blankets, wanting nothing more than to feel him overtop her once more. This was just taking too damned long.

Her panties released from her toes and suddenly, he was back, every inch of skin bare and perfect. She ran her hands through his thick, wild hair, her fingers brushing against his pointed ears, which flicked each time she touched them. Meanwhile, he rubbed their lower bodies together, sending her anticipation soaring.

"Now," she said, pulling on his hair.

"Absolutely." He didn't hesitate, joining them slowly but steadily.

Victoria couldn't help squirming, wanting to move but compressed under his weight. He needed to get on with it already. More than anything, she wanted to get to the good parts. She wanted her heart pounding in time with his, wanted to lose herself in the moment, in their connection.

Victoria pressed her hips up against his, curling her legs around his ass and her arms around his shoulders. She leaned in and nipped at his ear. "What are you waiting for?"

He groaned, the sound vibrating through her chest. He started moving, but his movements were erratic, like he couldn't quite control himself. She squeezed down hard on him, trying to see how far she could push him.

"Does this do it for you?"

She nodded, then gasped as he rubbed perfectly against her clit. Her entire body was on fire, practically screaming its pleasure. "Yes." Her voice was breathy, unrecognizable. "God, yes." Her head fell back on her neck, hanging in mid air as he held her close.

"Good."

He seemed to know exactly what he was doing, tweaking his technique as he went, just as attentive and observant inside the bedroom as out. She could barely breathe, barely hold a thought. Her body felt tight as a bowstring, screaming and reaching for something just out of reach.

It broke and her whole body went lax, her mind and body floating on a cloud as he sought his own release. His body went stiff in climax, a coughed animalistic noise forced itself from his lungs before he collapsed against her. They didn't move, sweat sticking their bodies together, chilling their skin and ardor.

"That was…"

"Mmm…" Victoria wasn't sure if she was completing his sentence or mindlessly making noise. Her brain still didn't seem capable of holding a thought, and her entire body felt like jello.

It felt wonderful.

This was a good idea.

"Ahem," someone interrupted.

It took her fried brain a moment to recognize the voice. She tensed, glaring up at the ceiling as her euphoria was invaded. "Angus, what the fuck?!"

"Apologies, but there is a ship within visual range."

CHAPTER TEN

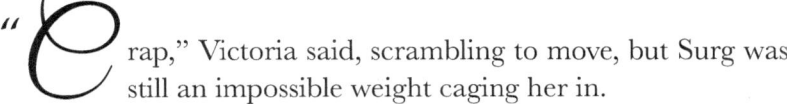

"Crap," Victoria said, scrambling to move, but Surg was still an impossible weight caging her in.

"Hey," he said, caressing her cheek. "We've got time. Relax."

She stilled. "Relax? They're here. We need to get moving." She squirmed to get out from under him but froze when his body automatically reacted. Her eyes widened, and her voice squeaked out of her. "You have a good recovery time."

Surg sighed and lifted up off her, reaching out a hand to help her off the bed. "Do humans not?"

She shook her head. *I can do this. This isn't awkward at all.* "Not really sure. Women often have fantastic recovery times, but I've heard men don't. Like it can take them a half hour."

"Half hour?"

"Um, that would be… about fifteen diceros?"

He nodded and grabbed his clothes. She couldn't help watching him as he pulled on his pants, her body refusing to turn away as she backed up to to her dresser, where clean clothing waited. She tried to get dressed herself, but her distraction and rush to act defeated her. First, her feet got tangled in the legs of her pants. Then, as if to add to her frustration, her head snagged on her shirt, seemingly unable to find the right hole. Anxiety over the coming events returned with lightning speed, eradicating the high she'd just been on.

"Hey," he said, helping her fix her shirt. When she was properly dressed, he rubbed her sides. "It's fine. We planned this. We've got Cass, Kou, and Jessie at our backs. The bad guys won't know what hit them."

She nodded, and he stepped away. "Angus, inform Cass of incoming. Victoria, we need to get geared up."

"Yes, sir," Angus said overhead.

Victoria reached out and grabbed Surg's hand, letting him lead her into her laboratory. With her mind focused inward, locked onto her anxiety, she didn't see any of the intervening distance. Nor did she really hear Surg coordinating efforts with Angus. She knew they were talking, but it was like they weren't actual words.

What if there's more than we thought?

What if we're outnumbered, underprepared?

Her mind kept cycling through what ifs, torturing herself with worst-case scenarios.

As they entered her lab, she imagined Surg laying bleeding out on the floor. She stopped, couldn't move forward. Her body felt numb, detached. She could barely breathe.

I can't do this.

Surg turned as Victoria came abruptly to a stop. "Victoria?" She almost looked like a doll staring off into the distance. "Hey, hey, what's wrong?" He cupped her face, but she just flinched, pulling away.

He stopped and stepped back. Touching her was clearly the wrong approach. Looking behind him, he spotted the protective gear Cass had given them when she arrived. Taking another glance at Victoria, he backed up again, watching her carefully as he pulled on body armor and weapon harnesses.

It was eerie, watching her, almost like a robot in standby mode. He'd never seen a person do that, not once in his life. The only approximation he could draw was animals freezing in the presence of a predator. Was she reacting to a threat?

Finished suiting up, he grabbed the gear intended for Victoria and approached her. When he held the pile out to her, she took them and started putting them on, but her movements seemed off, like she wasn't completely there.

"Come on," he said as she finished. She followed sedately, and he ushered her into the hiding place they'd chosen. It provided good cover and would allow him to return fire.

In his mind, he imagined the scenario. From here, he could see the airlock. They would pour through, armed to the teeth. He would open fire from behind the door, his body between them and Victoria.

Time passed by in slow increments.

Surg couldn't decide on the best way to proceed. Should he keep a gun in his hand? Should he stay on alert? Or should he relax while he could, let Angus warn them when enemy contact was imminent?

Suddenly, Angus's voice filled the room, taking the decision away from him. "Prepare for boarding."

CHAPTER ELEVEN

*S*urg tensed, lifting his gun to the ready. The air seemed to still in the wake of Angus's words. His breaths were too fast in the small space, and he became hyper-aware of even the slightest movement, the slightest sound.

He could hear Victoria behind him, her breaths puffing out of her. She didn't sound scared or panicked, which he took as a blessing.

He slipped to the side, aiming his barrel at the airlock door, ready to pull the trigger the moment it opened. He was tempted to hold his breath. It felt like time stood still, dragging out into infinity, as he waited for the imminent attack. Would they storm in like a flood, trying to scare their target with a show of force? Or would they be more careful, checking the ship methodically until they achieved their goal?

He didn't have long to wait. The airlock door lifted with a whoosh, and an armed man stepped through in a crouch, his head barely clearing the bottom of the door. Surg fired.

The sound reverberated in the room. While it was quieter than some models, it still pierced his ears in the confined space, causing them to twitch. Victoria whimpered and shifted behind him. Surg tried to ignore her, to focus on the problem, but it was hard. He wanted to turn around and comfort her, but there would be no comforting until this was over.

The man he'd shot was sprawled in the open doorway. Agitated words drifted back and forth, quiet enough that Surg couldn't understand them. The barest edge of someone peeked out from their hiding place, but not enough for a clear shot.

No, the only thing he could see was that body. Blood was sprayed across the walls with bone and brain matter mixed in, making him want to throw up. He'd never killed anyone before. There was a part of him that was feeling increasingly numb. He still breathed, still held the gun gripped in his hands, still watched that gruesome tableau, but something felt wrong, adrift. Surg had always prided himself on above board tactics. He hated the Diehli for the way they conducted business. He'd always seen that as the perfect example of how *not* to do things. To be here, now, felt like an ultimate failing, like he'd betrayed his principles.

I killed a man.

A gun barrel and part of an arm peeked out around the doorframe. Surg fired again. The round hit the metal, melting it slightly, and the arm retreated. He looked down at the gun, surprised that he'd pulled the trigger again.

What have I become?

And how long did he have to hold out until Cass arrived?

"Come *on*, sis. What's taking so long?"

Cass looked away from the control panel to glare at her little sister. "Cool it, Jess. If you keep interrupting me, it'll never get done." She didn't usually initiate a hack remotely. It was far easier to compromise a ship in dock. She had access to the hardware that way. It was a gamble whether this would work. Still, she could pull it off so long as she could connect with the right systems.

Just not comms. People expected that. No, if this was going to work, she needed to use a system people didn't expect to be compromised. Like navigation.

Most navigation systems were linked to a remote database, allowing it to be automatically updated with new information as needed. Since those updates were usually externally triggered, she just needed to learn the type of ship to know how to force an "update."

"Done!" She leaned back in triumph.

"That's it?" Jess scoffed.

"Just give it time." Cass stood from her seat. "In the meantime, we need to get ready to breach. Angus? Initiate approach as soon as their sensors are offline." Because the target ship would be attached to the *Discovery*, she'd needed to rethink her plan this time. She couldn't drop oxygen levels on the ship without affecting Surg and Vicky as well. And since atmospherics on the *Discovery* were still active, it wouldn't be nearly as effective. She'd nixed the idea of turning off atmospherics on the *Discovery* since it might alert their prey that something was awry.

No, this time, she'd taken advantage of the enemy crew's plans to board another ship. With their focus elsewhere, she'd turned off their sensors so she, Kou, and Jess could board the enemy ship without the crew knowing.

Cass and Jess crossed the *Trojan* in moments. When they entered the cargo bay, Kou was already there, covered in body armor and weaponry. Cass smiled. "God, I just want to tackle you right now."

"Focus," he said, tossing her a weapons belt.

She started securing it in place, reassured by its weight. She crossed the room and loaded up with the rest of her gear.

"Prepare for alterations in gravity," Angus said.

Cass gripped the counter next to her, and she watched as Kou and Jess took similar stances. She didn't know what would happen next. Usually, docking meant a loss of gravity as the rotation of the ship was instrumental to the gravity systems, but the enemy ship had docked with the *Discovery* while it was still rotating, meaning they had to hit a moving target. Angus could do it, but she had no idea what would happen. They'd never done it before.

"Uh," she said as her stomach seemed to dip and rise. Gravity disappeared for a moment, then reasserted itself with a jarring intensity. "Damn," she said as everything returned to normal. She was on her knees, her hand still gripping the counter above her.

"Connection established. Sealing gateway." Angus's voice filled the room, creating a sense of urgency.

The three of them moved to the airlock door. Cass gripped the gun at her hip, waiting impatiently.

Come on…

The door hissed open, and she pulled her gun, rushing through. She felt a little like she was playing a game.

Game… Set… Match.

As expected, the ship appeared empty. No one met them at the door. She used the bracer on her wrist to guide her through the ship.

The interior looked nothing like the *Trojan*, and not just because Jess had painted the hallways with murals. Here, the walls were made of metal, but dark, setting a mood for a tragic ending. The doors they passed were a different shape than she was accustomed to, a little taller and a lot wider. She held up a hand as they approached the next corner. Angus had been running heat scans, and there didn't seem to be any stray life-forms on the ship except at the airlock up ahead. When they turned the corner, they would be exposed.

She pulled up the enemy's surveillance system. It took a moment to find the camera she wanted. The angle was poor, not intended for her purposes. A handful of men of indeterminate species stood in the space between two doors. They were at the very edge of the camera's range. She couldn't tell how well armed they were, only their number. Even including Surg and Vicky in the other ship, they were outnumbered.

Cass smirked, her body relaxing. She liked those odds. All the men were facing away from them. She motioned Kou to move to the opposite corner. It would give them more cover.

Bringing her weapon back up to her shoulder, she signaled a countdown.

3

2

1

Cass peeked out around the corner and opened fire. She didn't bother to aim. Kou fired as he crossed to the opposite side of the doorway. Two bodies dropped to the floor and several more grunted as they were hit.

Chaos erupted in front of her, the men yelling and scrambling to find cover, but there just wasn't enough space. They needed to take cover from three different angles, and it just wasn't possible.

She continued to fire, this time more targeted. She was patient, waiting until she had a decent target. One by one, their enemy dwindled. They'd started the firefight outnumbered, but they were in a far superior position and location was everything. Panic slowly filled the airlock as the men trapped there realized the futility of their situation. They fired blindly, and Cass pulled back, watching as the rounds started melting the wall in front of her, the only target their enemy had. Her heart pounded with the sound, but she wasn't afraid. It was the last ditch effort of people with no hope of victory.

"Stand down. Drop your weapons," she yelled in a rare moment devoid of gunfire.

Cass waited. Seconds passed, her finger still pressed hard and ready against the outside of the metal trigger guard. Finally, a gun clattered to the floor. Another followed, then the last two remaining men stepped out, hands far out to their sides in surrender.

"Move." She pointed with her gun. She and Kou guided them through the airlock and into the *Discovery*. She had to step over guns and bodies. "On the ground, now."

Beyond the two men, Surg stood next to a door he'd clearly used for cover. The metal was dented, with scorch marks from non-physical rounds.

"You okay?" Cass's throat was tight. Where was Vicky? Was she okay? Was she deeper in the ship? She couldn't imagine the gentle designer taking part in a firefight, and she wouldn't be satisfied until she saw Vicky was safe with her own eyes.

"Yeah." He looked behind him, then back at her. "I kept her safe. All clear?"

Cass nodded. "All clear."

Victoria spent a while in that closet even after the fighting stopped. All her nerves were shot, vibrating with the energy of the moments leading up to that one. When she could finally pull herself together, she was tired, exhausted, and she didn't really want to leave the small room. She'd heard Cass, Kou, Jessie, and Surg talking back and forth, letting their voices wash over her as they dealt with the mess just outside her line of sight. She didn't want to know, didn't want to see.

When she stepped around the door, blood smeared the walls, but only Surg remained in the room.

"You feeling better?" he said.

She nodded, still a little too fragile to speak.

"The others are on the enemy ship. They've set up a room to interrogate them. Do you want to come with?"

She nodded again and followed Surg through the carnage at the airlock. It was going to take a lot of cleaning and repairs to get the ship back up to snuff. She was tempted to run her fingers over the wall, but it was covered with blood, and she shivered. She watched the wall instead of Surg, looking for spots clear of body fluids.

When they exited the airlock, she touched the clean wall's surface. It was slightly textured, and she focused on that as she tracked Surg's movements in her peripheral vision. She didn't know where they were going, but did it matter? She wasn't sure she had the brainpower to make decisions right now, anyway.

The wall fell away, and they stepped into a large open area. Crates and boxes were strapped against the far wall, and two men were tied to chairs in the middle of the room.

"Glad you could join us."

Victoria glanced over at Cass, who stood in front of the seated men, fists on her hips and jacket hanging open. She looked like a badass, but then she was one.

Meanwhile, I just curled up in a ball like a wimp...

Shame teased her as she stood on the outskirts, waiting for answers. Would they get them? Did these men know why she was being chased? Did they know who was behind it?

Surg touched her shoulder, then moved up beside Cass. A beat of silence hovered over the room. Victoria honestly couldn't imagine what they might plan to do to these people. They were in the middle of nowhere, outside the jurisdiction of any government. They could do whatever they wanted with these men, and no one could punish them for it.

But she trusted Cass, believed in her. Sure, she was a pirate, she held no illusions about that, but she also knew her friend. For all her bravado, she never wanted to hurt people. With her skills, she could just as easily kill all the beings on board and steal the ship itself, but she never did that. She always left the crew unharmed. Sometimes, they didn't even know they'd been robbed.

In fact, she couldn't help wondering if today had been the first time Cass had killed someone. She seemed strong, untouched by the events of the day, but was she? Was she just putting on an act? Victoria used to be pretty good at reading body language, but she was awfully rusty, having lived so long alone. Could she be missing some vital clue? Or maybe it hadn't hit her friend yet, and it would hit her like a ton of bricks later?

"This is going to go very simple. We want to know one thing. If you tell the truth, good things happen to you. If you lie or hide things from us, bad things happen to you." Cass leaned in the face of one of the men, then the other. Kou loomed behind her like some ominous monster, his war wounds a cybernetic warning of what he was capable of. Beside them, Surg stood with his back to Victoria, arms crossed over his chest, standing tall and confident. His body language spoke of command, power.

One of the seated men spat at Cass while the other sat mostly still, but a small movement gave him away. *He* was the one who would crack first. Should she tell them? Did they already know?

Victoria zoned out as the interrogation continued. It seemed to consist of a lot of questions, aggressive displays, and posturing... on both sides. She glanced over at Jessie, who was leaned against the wall picking her nails and yawning.

Then Angus spoke up from the bracer on Cass's wrist. "I've identified their likely point of origin. This ship has made routine trips, going back for years, to the headquarters of Dielhi, your rival, Surg."

Surg cursed, and Victoria snapped out of her stupor, stepping up closer to the others.

Surg's head sagged, his ears flicking agitatedly. "Of course, it's them. Who else would it be?"

"What's going on? Who is Dielhi?" Victoria said.

Surg shook his head, pulling himself up straight again. "Not who, what. Diehli is a very corrupt company that my company has butted heads with more times than I can count. They'll do anything to get what they want, and I just can't abide by that."

"Your… company?"

He looked over at her. "Yeah, Inia Intergalactic."

For a moment, Victoria couldn't move, couldn't think, unable to reconcile the man she'd come to know, even slept with, with the reality she was now confronting.

"Vicky, you didn't know that? I *work* for this guy," Cass said, pointing a thumb at Surg.

Victoria bristled at the nickname, but shook her head in response. "No, you don't. You work for yourself. You always have."

Cass nodded her head. "Until a few months ago, when I met Kou. I'm more privateer than pirate now."

"What?" Victoria's memories and fears were rushing back at her, things she thought she'd left behind years ago. All the times she'd been pushed to make a deadline even though she was just a kid, even though there were laws. All the times she'd been hounded by government, military, and corporations who wanted to work with her. Emails, phone calls, people in suits at their door. The feeling like the whole world was closing in on her. Her anxiety spiking every time she got a new email, her phone rang, or someone knocked on the door. Running and hiding in her room to escape, trying to pretend those triggers didn't exist, that there wasn't someone at the door, that there wasn't someone calling.

Her parents hadn't protected her. They'd let it happen. In fact, they'd reveled in the attention. She supposed, after years of watching her struggling with her grades, rarely making friends, never putting herself out there, seeing people value her must have felt nice to them. She'd certainly been worthless before that. Sometimes, she suspected her teachers had given her a passing grade because they didn't want to deal with her for a second year.

It was only after emancipation, after moving in with Cass and Jessie, that things had started to change. Although, at first, it hadn't been enough. She'd still been hounded. They'd found her, even in Cass's small apartment, even at school. Men in suits would show up, pull her out of class, and try to entice her to design something for them, to work for them. It was all smiles and bonuses and incentives, but it always triggered her fight-or-flight response. If she could have, she would have run and never stopped.

Without conscious thought, she started to back up, putting distance between herself and this reality she just couldn't handle. She shook her head, her hands vibrating at her sides. Past and present started to blend together. "No... No..."

"Victoria? Vic?"

She shook her head, started banging her temples with the heels of her hands. It didn't hurt, but it distracted her.

I need to escape.

Her breathing started becoming labored, her body tensing with memories she'd sooner forget. She needed an out. She couldn't be here. Not now. She needed to...

Run.

CHAPTER TWELVE

This isn't happening.

Victoria paced her room. She was overwhelmed, falling apart. She wanted to scream, to throw things. Her entire body felt completely out of control, screaming at her to *move*. But each movement only ramped her up even higher, pushing her to a breaking point.

He's a businessman. Just like them. Just like all of them.

She tried to keep her mind blank, but the memories and anxieties rose up like a tsunami. She pushed them back, but she wasn't sure if she was strong enough. Her memory was spotty at best and most times it was a good thing. It meant she didn't hold grudges. It meant she forgot about past traumas so they didn't consume her.

But that revelation had just brought it all back up to the surface.

Bang. Bang.

She jumped, standing in the middle of the room like a deer in the headlights, trying to decide whether to run.

"Vicky? It's me, Cass. Are you okay?"

She shook her head. "Just leave me alone."

I need to be alone.

The air hung with anticipation. Victoria could practically feel her friend waiting on the other side, deciding whether to intervene.

Just go away.

"Okay, Vicky. But I'm here if you need me."

Victoria let out a breath of relief. For a moment, the pressure she felt eased, then what she'd been battling smacked her in the face.

What if he's like all the rest?

He'll just take advantage of you.

What if he just wants your research?

What if it's all an act to get what he wants?

What if you're missing something important?

You know you always find out too late.

The last thought hit hard, and she gasped. She dropped to the floor, breathing heavily and sweating as the Generalized Anxiety Disorder she thought she'd overcome years ago snuck up on her with a vengeance.

It had taken being diagnosed with GAD at sixteen to snap her out of the cage everyone had created for her. She'd always loved spaceships, loved science and mechanics. She'd become obsessed at an early age, and her parents had encouraged her passions. Even though she was still in school, she'd developed revolutionary designs that corporations and government had scrambled to get their hands on.

Her parents had been so proud, lapping up the attention. So had Victoria, at first. She'd loved talking to the engineers, sharing her excitement, talking in a language that everyone else simply didn't understand.

But the attention soon became too much. She would throw a fit when people pushed her too far, then her parents would push her further, chastising her for the tantrum. She couldn't take it. Her parents kept encouraging her, promising things she couldn't or didn't want to accomplish. They pimped her out wherever they could, never seeing the danger in it.

They never wanted you. They just wanted the money.

She'd called the helpline herself, telling the person on the other end about her problems, her stresses, her thoughts. That had led to seeking a psychiatrist. It was probably the first time in two years that her parents had put her wellbeing over their own desires.

Therapy, coping techniques, and medication had helped, but it had also given her the first moment of clarity in quite a long time. Her parents saw her treatment as a way of helping her cope with the life she had. It taught *her* that she was trapped, that she needed to escape. So long as she was under her parents' thumbs, she would suffer with this disorder.

Except her father was Chinese. She was born in America, but some things were really important to him. Family was one of them. It was a virtue he had instilled on her as well. It was hard for her to accept the dichotomy that family, the very thing that was supposed to help and support you, was the thing tearing her apart. Her mother, from a devout Christian family that was just as close in their own way, had encouraged those strong familial bonds. It had been a noose and comfort in her younger years. There was something soothing about knowing you were part of a greater whole, but it could also put you in a terrible spot. Sometimes, no amount of encouragement, work, or sacrifice on your family's part would ever mold you into the person they wanted you to be.

She was smart, but struggled in school because she wasn't interested and couldn't focus. When she showed an interest in spaceships, her father was elated. He always encouraged her education, but all she wanted to do was learn about spaceships, nothing more. If it couldn't relate to them in any way, she wasn't interested. For years, they struggled. Her mother worked from home part time so she could work with Victoria and help her with her schooling, trying to get her interested and engaged. It worked some, at least. She did the best she could to link every subject back to spaceships. With math, they would add or subtract them. With English, they would read about them. With Science, they would discuss how various things might lead to their invention or creation. History was hardest. Far too much just couldn't be related to her favorite topic.

Those were the good days. It was hard, but she'd felt heard, like her mother accepted her and was willing to support her. She'd scraped by in school because of those lessons. Looking back, her mother during her elementary school years and her mother when she was sixteen were like two entirely different people. In her head, she often saw them as separate because she just couldn't reconcile the differences to herself.

It took therapy to finally realize her childhood version of her mother was gone. Her father, who had always been loving and supportive, was gone. Victoria couldn't return to the way things used to be. She might value family, might want that unconditional support, but she had to make a choice. She could either have a family that was hurting her, or she could start fresh and rebuild. Those were her options. She couldn't have it all.

So, she'd applied for emancipation and sued for the profits from her projects. Her parents had fought her. In court, they'd insisted she couldn't live on her own, quoting her disorder. She'd had to sit there listening as her parents demeaned her, tearing her apart. All throughout the proceedings, she remembered thinking, "I never want to see them again."

It was around the same time that she reconnected with Cass, Jessie, and Ellie. She'd met them all years before. This was before everything had gone all wrong. She'd never been the most social child, preferring to sit in her room reading technical manuals on ion propulsion engines rather than playing with other kids. Her parents had taken her to the park, but it didn't go well at first. Victoria had just wanted to go home. It was bright, loud, and most of the surfaces were either hot, abrasive, or pinched her skin. Cass was twenty. Her sister, Jessie, was seven. Cass had already been taking care of her full time. Ellie had run away from her school after a fiasco.

Victoria couldn't really say what had drawn them together. She'd been pushing herself on the swing, enjoying the back-and-forth momentum. It was soothing. When Ellie had rushed in, Cass had noticed the fifteen-year-old and went over to ask if she was all right. Jessie had trailed behind her, and Victoria had been momentarily pulled out of her head by Ellie's appearance. She'd worn a school uniform, the shirt pulling out of her waistband in places, one sock falling down around her ankle, but that wasn't what had drawn her attention. The girl's skin was purple. As she'd watched, the girl had tried to pull herself together, her skin tone shifting to a lighter tan, but she'd struggled, and it didn't hold, making her even more agitated.

Victoria had dragged her feet on the ground, kicking up the rubber mulch as she slowed to a stop. She'd crossed the space, watching as Cass tried and failed to soothe her. Jessie had seemed curious, popping her head out from behind Cass's arm and smiling.

"It's okay," Victoria had told the then stranger, Ellie. "You can feel what you want."

Snapped out of her fit, Ellie had turned to her. "Hi."

Victoria had tried to smile, but she'd never been very good at it. She couldn't count the number of photos where her smile had resembled a grimace. "Been there."

"Yeah?"

She'd nodded.

And that was the start of a friendship that continued to this day. During the court proceedings, she'd relied on her friends, friends she'd rarely seen in the craziness her parents had put her through. By then, both Cass and Ellie were adults. They'd stood up for her in the hearings, offering her places to stay, giving her hope.

She'd won her freedom, and with that freedom, she'd dived into ship design and building. She hadn't thought once of the financial implications, about profits. All she'd thought about was escaping. She'd still been taking her meds, still following her doctor's suggestions, and had escaped that toxic environment, but a part of her had still expected to be sucked back into that world. She'd half expected her parents to appear around every corner.

And, unfortunately, escaping her parents didn't mean she'd escaped the corporations and governments that still wanted her skills. They'd hounded her, harassed her. Her friends were protective, but they couldn't protect her from everything. And every time she was harassed, she'd buried herself deeper in her work, needing that escape.

She kept fantasizing about building a spaceship and escaping all the pressures of Earth, just fly away and never look back. But she couldn't bear the idea of leaving her friends behind, so when she'd developed her ship, she'd decided to make three of them. And they all contributed in their own ways. Cass had designed the AI, Angus, much to Ellie's chagrin.

Victoria smiled. Ellie *still* had trouble understanding Angus's accent.

Ellie had programmed Uso into the systems, including installing an educational program. There were a lot of species out there, but most used Uso as a universal language. It was the language of a peacekeeper race, a neutral party.

It wasn't until she first felt the *Discovery* take off from Earth that she felt the final vestiges of her disorder slip away from her. No more voicemails from her parents. No more suited men showing up at her door. No more emails proposing projects for her to work on.

She rubbed her forehead, trying to push all of that away. That was her past. Over. This was now, but it didn't feel that way. It felt like the past and present were merging, fusing together. She took a deep breath and let it out. She just needed time and space.

Unfortunately, she could practically *feel* the others on her ship, *feel* the pressure of their expectations.

She just wanted everyone to leave. She wanted to be alone.

Why couldn't they just leave her alone?

———

Surg leaned against the edge of the wall in the kitchen with Cass seated on the counter across from him. Kou and Jessie were back on the other ship with their prisoners, keeping an eye on them.

"You should talk to her."

Is she kidding? Doesn't she know her friend at all?

He shook his head. "That's not a good idea."

"She needs you to explain things." She slapped the counter, the sound echoing off the walls in the tiny room.

"Cass, drop it. She'll come around."

Cass scowled at him. "Why are you acting like this? She needs someone to slap some sense into her."

He stared at Cass, incredulous, but looking at her, he suspected her words were more frustration than anything else. Knowing the two of them well now, he couldn't imagine two friends who were more polar opposites. Cass was a take charge personality, rushing in almost recklessly. Victoria, on the other hand, tended to draw away from the world, preferring to do things at her own speed, in her own time. She'd probably spent years on this ship alone, while Cass had lived with her little sister. And it wasn't just the living situation that made them different, either. Cass was always the one to call Victoria, not the other way around, expressing an essential strategy in how they approached other people.

Did that make Cass right, though? He started to question his own approach. *Should* he make the first move, reach out to her? She might never reach out on her own. She might simply retreat, perfectly content to just let go of what they had.

I don't want that.

He tensed, hating the idea of giving up on this barely formed relationship they had. It was nothing, barely even a one-night stand, but he hadn't felt lonely or alone once since boarding her ship. Even when she was quiet, off in her own world, there was a comfort in her presence.

But was he projecting his own wants and needs onto Victoria? Was he letting them color and shape his conclusions? He didn't think so. Cass might be right that when Victoria was ready, it would probably take him making the first move, but she needed to be ready first. He didn't think she was yet.

"Gah, I hate doing nothing." Cass jumped off the counter, distracting Surg from his thoughts. "I'm gonna go talk to her. I'll break her door down if I have to."

"No, she needs her space."

He had to remind himself of that. He remembered their earlier encounters. Right from the beginning, he'd seen it. She might pull away at first, but she came around in her own time. And he felt confident that if he pushed her before she was ready, she would never forgive him.

Cass was frustrated. She didn't like sitting still, didn't like watching people she cared about suffer. For now, she was avoiding the prisoners, because she was afraid she would take out her frustrations on them, which would be unfair and counterproductive.

The frustration was getting to her, though, tensing her muscles, making her jaw clench, leaving her shoulders high and tight. As she'd said to Surg earlier in the day, she was very much tempted to try to break down Vicky's door, but she knew better. She wasn't *that* far gone. The door was far too sturdy. And she would never use that type of explosive ordinance on a spaceship.

Also, Vicky would probably kill her.

Well, no, she wouldn't, but she would certainly be pissed.

Maybe I should. It might break her out of this funk.

She shook herself, trying to loosen her tight muscles. She needed to act soon, or she might do something drastic.

Like break down Vicky's door.

Stop being ridiculous.

Cass should just go back to her ship, get some sleep maybe. There was no reason for her to be pacing a hole in the floor of her friend's lab. It felt wrong seeing it vacant. Every time she'd ever been in here, Vicky had been sitting at that workstation. All her gear was there, a bunch of high-tech equipment Cass couldn't even fathom, but it didn't have the same chaotic edge it usually did. Why?

It looks tidied. Boarded up.

That was it. There were no papers sitting out, no tablet sitting on the counter, half hanging off with the screen still on. There were no active experiments. Usually, there was the noise of one piece of equipment or another humming or singing in the background. The room was silent except for the gentle hum of the ship's engines and the whoosh of rushing air through the vents.

Cass's heart hurt at the realization. She'd known pretty early on that Vicky needed her work. She was obsessed. Cass had, at first, thought her friend would quit once she escaped her parents, no longer pressured to perform, but she didn't. Even when she no longer had to, she still sat up at night reading white papers, textbooks, and scientific journal articles. It was like she couldn't help herself.

At first, Cass had thought Vicky was a genius. After all, here she had a sixteen-year-old under her roof reading journal articles probably written for people with PhDs. Vicky had routinely chattered excitedly about new things she'd learned, leaving Cass's head spinning. She'd found undergraduate and graduate level textbooks lying around the apartment. But it hadn't taken long for her to realize that it was all passion. Like Cass with her programming, she didn't have to be smart to get good at something she enjoyed. She was certain Vicky was smart, probably smarter than herself, but she was no genius. She struggled in almost every facet of life. Except one… her passion.

So, as Cass looked at the space around her, it was almost as if Vicky had packed up and left, like she was leaving, maybe never to come back.

Behind her, a door clicked closed, and she turned around, expecting to find Surg leaving his room, but it was Vicky.

Finally.

She held her breath, keeping herself mostly concealed behind the doorframe, not wanting to spook her friend. She felt a little like a hunter not wanting to startle its prey.

Cass watched as Vicky moved toward her down the hallway, then slipped into the galley.

Now's my chance.

Cass stepped forward, moving silently along the metal floor, which wasn't an easy accomplishment. She stopped right before entering the room, still out of sight. Surg's words caused her to hesitate for a moment.

Was he right? Should she leave Vicky alone? Would that be better? She didn't want to hurt her friend or make things worse, but she couldn't bear not knowing. What had set Vicky off like that? Why had she run? They had just started getting answers when Vicky had suddenly bailed, rushing back to her ship without a backward glance. Why would she do that? It didn't make any sense.

It reminded Cass of when she'd first offered Vicky a place to stay. She'd been suing her parents for emancipation. She'd been suffering an anxiety disorder and could no longer hide the toll the experience was having on her. Cass had watched as that shy girl who'd said just the right thing to the fragile Ellie years earlier struggled to do absolutely anything.

The court battle had been an uphill struggle. Vicky's parents had so much on their side. Their daughter's mental illness, her "complicated" finances. They'd claimed that Vicky couldn't support herself on her own. But eventually, the testimonies had built up, and the tides had shifted. Cass and Ellie had both offered her a home, offering to help her get on her feet. And the psychiatrist had even admitted that she suspected Vicky's home environment was contributing to her mental illness. She'd suggested a less stressful environment would be more conducive to her recovery.

The psychiatrist had been right. After the battle was over, Vicky had settled in quite nicely. She was closer in age to Jess than Cass, and after a while, Vicky had started helping Jess with homework or playing games with her, though the games had to be carefully curated. Mostly, Cass had to throw out any games that required too much strategy. Vicky always won games like checkers and Chinese checkers, while she would throw fits and eventually refused to play chess.

Before long, she felt like a part of the family, and Cass completely forgot about the anxiety disorder. Vicky talked animatedly about things she learned and shared designs for ship components, even though Cass couldn't have said what any of them were. They all encouraged her. It was nice seeing her so alive.

She'd never expected to see that broken girl again, but as she peeked into the galley, Vicky stood in front of the robot. It whirred as it cooked her food. Vicky was tense, her hands shaking at her sides. Her body was hunched in slightly on itself. For a moment, she considered just walking away, but she'd never walked away from a challenge in her life. She hadn't walked away years ago when Vicky had needed her, and she wasn't about to start now.

She leaned against the door frame, arms crossed over her chest. "What's going on, Vicky?"

Vicky tilted her head toward Cass, but didn't really look at her. "Just… leave me alone. Please."

"No. Tell me what's going on. I can't help you if you don't speak up."

Vicky looked her in the face finally, but Cass could see how much effort it was to pull off. "You can't help."

"Yes, I can. I'm your friend. When have I *not* been there for you?" She dropped her arms and took a step into the room.

Vicky tensed and looked away. "That's not the point."

"Then what is?" She decided to change tactics. "What caused you to run?"

"It doesn't matter."

"Bullshit."

Vicky jerked, looking at her once more. "Just drop it."

"No. I'm not going to let you retreat like this." She moved farther forward as she spoke, not even realizing it. "You've come so far. You're not that little girl anymore."

Vicky creeped backward, looking up at Cass, but this time, while her mouth opened, no words came out.

"Come on," Cass reached out, touching Vicky's shoulder. "Let me help you."

Vicky flinched and made a weird noise in her throat that spoke of fear and frustration before pushing past Cass and fleeing.

Cass turned to the doorway, but Vicky was already out of sight. "Damn."

Surg was right.

CHAPTER THIRTEEN

*S*urg had wanted to hit Cass when he found out she'd cornered Victoria in the kitchen. Victoria had rushed out without even getting food, which meant she was going without. Here, he'd been waiting patiently, and Cass just *had* to push her.

He'd been waiting for Victoria to reach out to Cass, Kou, or Jessie when she was ready. They were friends, after all.

Unlike me.

He was just an outsider, a stranger. And it was immediately after Angus mentioned Surg's company that Victoria had fled. He just *knew* that was the trigger, but how? He didn't know enough about her past to know what that might be.

Should he ask Cass or Jessie? They'd both known her longer. They might know what had set her off.

And yet… Cass had seemed equally dumbfounded. In spite of their friendship, she didn't know why that revelation had bothered Victoria so much.

Still, his best bet was to wait until she came out of her shell again.

Which left him with nothing to do, yet again. They hadn't moved since setting their trap, and they were being careful about outbound communications. Angus was continuing to investigate the Diehli ship's computers while Cass and Kou interrogated their prisoners. He didn't have the heart to help anymore.

Instead, he sat in the bedroom he'd been assigned with the door ajar, hoping to spot Victoria leaving her room. In the days that followed, he'd spotted her getting something to eat, but she'd always seemed skittish, immediately returning to her room with a plate of food.

He actually missed the busy, if impersonal, environment at Inia Intergalactic now. He'd had a specific role, and there was always something to do, always something to distract him from his moods. Here, he couldn't hide behind his work anymore. No, he had to face this head on. There was literally nothing else to do but think.

He wanted to say he'd made great accomplishments in his life so far, that he was proud of how far he'd come, but he wasn't really sure. Part of the reason for starting his business was so he and his younger brother never had to suffer the injustices of poverty ever again. But what had that gotten him? He remembered a time when he'd been close to his brother. They'd been friends. Beffa, Varn had helped him when starting his company. He'd been Surg's first employee.

And yet now, he rarely saw him. How long had it been? He couldn't even remember. How sad was that? Varn was his only family, and he couldn't even remember the last time they'd seen each other in person.

And the rest of his life was a great wasteland. He had no one he would stretch to calling a friend, and for some time now, his lack of companionship, his loneliness, had been hitting him hard.

I've done this to myself.

That thought shouldn't have been a revelation, but it was. He'd deluded himself for so long, convincing himself that everything he did was necessary, or that the elements he found lacking in his life could wait. But who was he kidding now? No one. Did anyone back at the office even notice his absence? He doubted it. Why would they? Like him, they were probably all absorbed in their own little lives, rarely escaping to see the world around them.

But what could he do? He felt trapped by the reality he'd built, which was probably why he felt so free on Victoria's ship. Maybe this had been his motivation for following that lead instead of calling in the team he'd assembled. Maybe he'd needed to get away, and that was the excuse he'd used to justify it to himself.

He supposed it didn't matter in the long run.

A lock disengaging jarred him out of his spiraling thoughts, and he snuck a peek through the gap in his door. Victoria stood gloriously in the halo of light coming from her room. She was dressed in another one of her casually comfortable outfits. Soft fabrics that made him want to explore them, then explore the soft skin beneath. Her long hair was pulled back at the base of her neck, something she hadn't done in days.

Hope sprang up inside him. He wanted to go to her, ask how she was doing, but he stayed in place, leaning out as she walked down the hallway, her back to him. He smiled when she passed the kitchen, heading toward her lab at the back of the ship.

He sighed.

Finally.

Victoria let out a sigh of relief when she reached her lab and still hadn't encountered anyone. Every time she'd left her room, she'd struggled with anxiety. She'd often stood with her hand on the handle, unable at first to turn it, to open the damned door. She'd half expected to be confronted the moment she stepped outside.

That little scene with Cass in the galley hadn't helped, either. She'd just wanted to get something to eat, and Cass had cornered her. In situations like that, all she'd ever wanted to do was escape, but Cass had never understood that. In the past, Victoria had dealt with Cass's approach to life by retreating to her room. Well, hers and Jessie's. At the time, Cass hadn't been able to afford more than a two bedroom. It was stifling, leaving her nowhere to go when she needed space to herself. Jessie had often picked up on that, fleeing their bedroom when she saw Victoria in a mood, but it had still been hard, just like now.

I just want everyone to go.

She wasn't used to having people on her ship. Usually, it only happened when her friends visited, and they never stayed for long, certainly never for days on end like this. It practically made her skin crawl.

Then why didn't it bother you with Surg staying here?

She stopped, frozen next to her workstation by that thought. Her fingers rubbed over the surface, focusing on the smooth texture, the way it felt against her skin. It didn't make sense. She *had* been fairly comfortable with Surg on her ship.

Up until the moment I discovered his lies, that is…

She sat down in her chair, looking over her unusually clean and sterile workspace. It was never like this. Even at her most organized, she had equipment sitting out, and her tablet set out to take notes. She liked things a certain way, but sometimes keeping them that way was hard. She would absentmindedly walk off with something, then forget where she left it. Or maybe she would be struggling with an especially difficult problem, and then the next thing she knew, she had things strewn everywhere, a perfect mirror of her mental state.

Actually, the room kind of reflected her mental state right now. Empty… waiting… ready. Everything was there, just waiting for work to resume, but there was certainly nothing going on right now. She was too exhausted for that. She just wanted to curl up on her bed and sleep.

Victoria looked back at the hallway, contemplating doing just that, but resisted. She felt a little raw and tired, but that didn't mean she could hide from the world forever.

Problem was, she wasn't sure what she *should* do. Her life had been in limbo since this all began, and she didn't know how to get anything started again.

"Hi," a breathy voice said from her right.

Victoria jerked, spinning to face the intruder. Cass had peeked her head through the airlock door, smiling ruefully.

"Sorry." She stepped out into the open. "Twice over, I guess. I shouldn't have cornered you like that. I'm sorry."

Victoria looked away, not sure what to say. What *could* she say? She'd always been bad at this sort of thing. Why was it so easy for everyone else? She shrugged and looked up.

"You doing better?" Cass asked, her shoulders hunched with her hands in her pockets as she shifted in place.

"Getting there."

Cass nodded. "Listen, I'm not gonna push. I know that was wrong, but I'll listen. Whatever you want to say, I'll listen. Or, if you don't want to talk, I can just be here... or walk away. Whatever you need."

"Thanks." Victoria didn't know what to do. Cass clearly expected something, but Victoria wasn't the type to just open up to others. Should she continue on the subject Cass had pressed earlier? It seemed the most likely topic to cover.

Why did I run? That's easy.

But talking about it wasn't. Had she ever had this conversation with Cass? She couldn't remember. She'd always been a little closer to Jessie. Jessie was a creator like herself, though Jessie's preferred medium was art, not ship design. They were also closer in age, separated by only a few years. It was part of the reason she'd moved in with Cass instead of Ellie. At the time, Ellie had been rebelling against her parents in any way she could. That meant she had an apartment which was often empty. Maybe it would have been easier for her, but Ellie had been a storm of emotions back then. Victoria had feared how that would affect her. Sometimes, other people's emotions could rile her up, and she'd already been on edge, barely holding it together.

So, as an explanation, she simply said, "Surg."

Cass rolled her eyes. "I kind of figured *that* part out."

"His business." Damn, she really didn't know how to say this. Only the two words came out, but they weren't enough. They could never encompass the depth of her feelings, her fear.

Cass didn't chime in this time, instead stepping forward and finding something to sit on. She just waited, probably for the first time in her life.

"You know about my emancipation, my anxiety disorder."

"Of course."

Victoria rubbed her face, her fingers ice cold against her heated cheeks. "I'm not sure where it went wrong. At first, I loved it. I loved working on creating these designs, these ships. I loved talking to people who felt just as passionate about it as I did." She shook her head. "But for corporations, it was never enough. The government jobs weren't so bad, although I'm not sure how I feel about the nature of the work. At the time, I was too young to really understand." She looked away, staring at the empty table next to her. "My parents were so proud. They preened on the attention I received.

"Before long, I had too many projects, too many deadlines. It was just too much." She stopped, unable to go on. That period in her life was a bit of a haze, blurred and shrouded in her anxiety, filled with these episodes and outbursts she barely remembered afterward. She remembered screaming and lashing out at someone, hiding in a little used room as she curled up on the floor, crying because she couldn't make an impossible deadline.

"After the emancipation, I thought I was free." She shook her head. "I wasn't. I was hounded by all those organizations that wanted my work. Emails, calls, showing up at our home in fancy suits. I couldn't escape it. They wouldn't take no for an answer. I changed every means of contact I could, but they always found me. Always."

Cass frowned. "And you associate that with… Surg?"

"Why wouldn't I? He's just like them."

"He's *nothing* like them. I know I'm probably about the most cynical bastard in existence, but you can trust him. He's not like that. And I think you know that. In all my dealings with him, he has always been fair. He's never done something unethical or immoral. When his opponents have done under-handed deeds, he's refused. Hell, he's the reason me and Kou are still together."

"What?"

"Yeah. Let's just say security specialist and pirate weren't exactly the most obvious of pairings at first." She smiled. "But damn, is it right. He seemed to really care about us. And he hired *me* to sort of keep the Diehli in check."

"The Diehli."

"Yeah, the company after you. It isn't exactly the first time we've had to deal with them. They are... shall we say... *not* averse to accomplishing things by questionable means. They're pretty much the worst, from what I gather. Most large companies out here, they set themselves up almost like govern-ments. They avoid territories of governing bodies so no one can oversee their activities, but they're still at the mercy of their clients and customers. Image is important, and that often keeps them in check... mostly.

"Not the Diehli, though. I'm not sure if they just don't care, or their customers are the type of people who appreciate that image, sort of like a barely veiled threat. Surg had been butting heads with them for a long time, certainly longer than we've worked for him. In fact, the job that had me meeting Kou actually involved both Surg and the Diehli."

"How?"

"I stole something Surg had contracted a group to discover, and the Diehli took a shortcut and tried to steal it. They were willing to kill for it."

"Crap."

"Yeah, exactly." Cass shook her head, looking a little deflated. "Listen, you have every right to how you feel. We all have our baggage, some heavier than others, but I really do think he's a good guy, so try not to let his title affect how you see him?"

She nodded, but it wasn't that easy. Could she simply look past years of reinforced impressions? She didn't know, and she hated herself a little for that.

Victoria turned back to her workstation, wanting a distraction. She didn't want to think about this anymore. If she spent too much time dwelling on it, she would just stress herself out all over again.

Better to distract yourself.

Except, all of her work was stowed away for safety. She didn't want the wrong person to get their hands on it, but they'd caught the guys responsible, right? Sure, there was a larger group working behind the scenes, but she should be able to work a *little*, right?

She pulled out her tablet, propping it up on the surface before her, and entered her credentials to view the encrypted data.

Surg watched Victoria from the hallway, feeling a bit like a creep. He wanted to regain her trust, get back to where they'd been, but he had no idea how to go about it. When she'd walked into her lab, he'd been torn between staying in his room to give her space and following just to be near her.

In the end, being her own personal stalker won out even while he mentally kicked himself for the behavior.

What had gotten into him?

Then Cass had shown up, and he couldn't have possibly antic-ipated what would happen next. He sagged against the wall while hearing Victoria retell her traumas, feeling like the worst scoundrel for listening in. It was obviously deeply personal, and he'd overstepped.

He turned his back on them in a daze, returning to his room and trying to close the door without a sound. He didn't want Victoria to know he'd heard, that he'd invaded her privacy like that.

Why did I do it?

It felt so out of character for him, made him question everything he thought he knew about himself. Like why he was still here on the *Discovery*. He could have easily called for a ride, gone back to work. He could have called an entire security force to look after Victoria, but he'd stayed enclosed in this small ship with her. Why?

Was it because of her? Or because of her discovery? Certainly, instantaneous travel would be an impressive boon for any businessman, but he just couldn't believe he would stay for that. It flew in the face of everything he'd ever believed about himself.

Didn't it?

And then there was his rival, the Diehli. He'd suspected but hadn't known the Diehli were involved until the interrogations, but he did now. How was that influencing his motivations? He'd always hated that company, hated everything they did.

But no matter what, that still left a young woman, an inventor, in the middle of all this, fragile and alone. He couldn't bear the idea of seeing her hurt. It was probably the most acceptable thought he had running through his brain at that moment.

So if he could just focus on that…

He stood up, opening the door and peeking out. Like almost always, the hall was empty. He hadn't heard anyone traverse it while he was engaging in self-flagellation in his room. Surg stepped carefully toward the lab, trying not to make a sound. Victoria sat in the same place he'd seen her before, this time hunched over a screen while a stylus ran over the surface.

Was she working?

Surg changed directions, heading toward the kitchen. Had she eaten anything so far today? Somehow, he doubted it, and he was fairly certain it was growing late. He selected two meals on the display, choosing a meal for her he'd seen her select before.

He stood back and waited, trying to come up with a game plan for their next encounter. What should he say? What *could* he say?

I'm sorry I didn't tell you who I am?

Had a moment ever come up to talk about professions? He wasn't sure. He'd introduced himself, told her his name, but it hadn't felt like the time to just spill out his job title. It felt tawdry, like grand standing.

In the background, the robot whirred away. Food sizzled as it cooked, but he didn't really pay attention. He didn't feel hungry, even though he suspected it had been as long since he'd eaten as it had for Victoria.

What am I going to say?

The robot spit out the two plates, and he picked them up in both hands, moving toward the lab. But when he reached the threshold, he hesitated, staring at Victoria, hard at work. He was a little afraid, his gut churning.

You can do this.

Surg stepped forward, his feet feeling like lead. It should have been a quick, short distance, but it felt like forever. Was it too soon for her? Could she forgive him for not being more open, more up front? Looking back, he couldn't point at a time where he could have told her. And empirically, nothing he'd done or said was wrong, but it felt wrong. In this moment, it felt very wrong. He felt like he'd betrayed her.

"Here," he said, placing her plate on the surface beside her tablet and backing away, giving her space as he always did. He felt like holding his breath, waiting for rejection.

She looked over at the plate, then over her shoulder at him. She chewed her lip, her hand moving reflexively to her chest just above her neckline. Her hand sort of shivered in the air, like she was trying to stop herself from doing something. "Why didn't you say?"

"It just didn't... flow." It sounded so stupid the moment the words left his mouth. Didn't flow? What did that even mean?

She frowned. "I don't understand."

He sighed and looked away. "I wasn't trying to hide anything from you. It just never felt like a natural progression of the conversation."

Victoria didn't respond immediately. She stared at him. He could see it out of the corner of his eye. "I get that. I get that a lot. I used to get yelled at for that." She gave him a lopsided smile.

Surg looked up, surprised the conversation had gone so well so far. "Like when?"

"I just... my brain always worked differently, so things other people thought were important didn't matter to me. So when I speak, I don't always associate things the way people want me to. I mean, my brain moves from topic to topic. It's smooth and logical, but everyone else seems to want to stick to one thing."

Surg nodded and walked forward, leaning against the counter-top. "Do you forgive me?"

She shrugged. "I don't think there's anything to forgive. It's not forgiveness that's the problem."

"Then what is?" He crossed his arms over his chest.

She looked him directly in the eye. There was an energy there. He could sense the work it took for her to maintain eye contact. He could sense she didn't want to. "I've just got to work through my issues, that's all."

"Okay." He paused. He felt the need to reach out to her, to connect with her, but didn't think he had the right. Not now. Maybe not ever. "I'm here for you," he said instead. "When you're ready." As he stared into her, he could see the strain continued eye contact was having. He could see the urge to escape rising inside her once more. "And look away if you need to. I don't want you to feel uncomfortable."

"Thanks." She smiled and looked down at the food he'd brought. Her shoulders relaxed, and she tapped the counter next to her, inviting him to stay.

He smiled back, feeling a weight lifting from his chest as he moseyed up beside her, enjoying her company in silence.

CHAPTER FOURTEEN

*S*urg sat with Cass and Kou in their ship. The interrogation was over. They needed to come up with a plan. He looked back toward the entrance of the ship, thinking of Victoria back in her lab. They'd made progress, he felt, but there was still a lot they needed to work out.

Unfortunately, it would have to wait. The Diehli were behind all the threats to Victoria, and he knew the bastards. They would stop at nothing. And they had Victoria in their sights.

"So, what do we do?" Cass said, looking at him and Kou for answers. They sat in a circle in her cargo area. The room was mostly big and empty, with her gear neatly organized on the wall behind her. "This isn't exactly my area of expertise. I usually go after single ships. Easy in and out, clear objectives, easy to get the information I need. This is an entire company, a big one."

"That's right," Surg said, taking a deep breath. "The Diehli have resources that would rival some governments."

"So, how do we fix this? How do we get them to back down, to leave her alone?" Cass crossed her arms, looking impatient.

"Like Surg said, think of them like a government." Kou settled a hand on Cass's thigh, a clearly unconscious attempt to settle her.

Surg smiled a little, happy they'd settled into their relationship so well, still taking comfort in it even under less than ideal circumstances. That was what he wanted, more than anything.

"What are you thinking, Kou?" Cass leaned forward, elbows on her knees.

"We treat this as we would a government. What would we do to make a government stand down?"

Surg leaned forward, getting back to the topic at hand. "Make the cost of engagement too high."

Victoria sat in her lab, working on an experiment. Normally careful, she was getting obsessive in her need to keep her data private and secure. Everything was encrypted. Her prototypes were under lock and key and only accessible by biometric access. She *needed* to do this, to get this right. Even with the Diehli breathing down her neck, she pushed herself further into her research, relying on its ability to help her escape from the mess of her life.

She knew the others were meeting to discuss things, to make a strategy. She'd registered them walking behind her earlier, leaving the ship. It had barely been a blip on her radar, just some movement out of her periphery, but she'd noticed. She knew they were making plans without her, but she didn't care.

"Hey," Surg said.

She looked up and over to the airlock, where he stood leaning against the doorjamb. "Hi," she said, dropping her hand from the prototype she was tweaking.

"Can we talk?"

Victoria nodded resignedly, pushing herself back from her workstation. She preferred to talk when she was working. She found that easier, but people expected differently. They always expected things that didn't come naturally to her, that were *hard* for her, but what could she do? "What's the plan?"

"Well, we haven't decided quite yet. We're gathering information still. Angus is going to try to pull information from Diehli headquarters using the hijacked ship and see if we can get a better idea of what we're dealing with. Once we do, I'm probably going to call in people from my company to help."

Victoria flinched, her body going tense, an automatic reaction to her teenage years when even her home wasn't safe from intrusion by those with power. Nowhere was. She stood, her body thrumming with nerves. "I gotta go." She turned her back on Surg, fleeing to her bedroom once more.

"Victoria, wait. What did I do this time?"

She stopped, her heart hammering away in her chest, hand tapping gently at her thigh. She wanted to tell him, but what could she say? Her feelings defied words and speech. They just felt overwhelming, like a tumor choking off her airway.

"What do you want me to do? Give it up? Give up my company? Would that make you feel safe? Because I can't change who I am." He pointed at his chest. "This is me. Me. A man who dragged himself and his brother out of poverty. Me. A man who's tried his best to be aboveboard in his tactics." He took a couple steps forward. "I want you to feel safe, to feel comfortable with me. Just give me a chance."

She wanted to. Oh, how she wanted to. But how?

———————

Cass sat in the cockpit of the *Trojan*. She hated waiting, hated doing nothing. She felt like time was slipping away from them, that they needed to act soon.

"We can't hold them indefinitely," Kou said from behind her.

She jumped, spinning in her seat. "Fuck, man. Don't scare me like that."

He didn't say anything, just stood there being his big, sexy self. She eyed him up and down and just wanted to lick him from head to toe, but it wasn't the time. They had more important things on the horizon, like the Diehli, like their prisoners.

"I know that," she said with a sigh. But she didn't have a plan, either.

On the one side, every moment they kept them and remained attached ship to ship, they were at risk. What if a distress beacon had been sent? What if not receiving any contact from the ship caused an automatic response? "We need to do something."

"I know."

She leaned against the seat back, her forearm digging into the stuffed leather. "Well, what do we do? You're the big combat veteran. What's your idea?"

He stepped into the room and sat down in the seat next to her. "The way I see it, these are the things we need to do, not necessarily in this order. First on the list, we need to temporarily disable the ship so it can't move or send communications and then move to a secondary location. They can't know where we are. Second, Surg can gather forces from his company to help us rescue Victoria. Third, if it were me, I would wipe all evidence of your friend from their records. They won't come after someone they don't know exists. Not sure if that needs to be done first or last. Will depend on if it can be done remotely or not."

"Angus, can we do it?" Cass looked up to the ceiling. She had some skills with hacking, but she was only human, and this was on an entirely different level. The central computer at Diehli headquarters would be a beast unlike anything she'd ever encountered, and IT security at a company like that would be insane. She would have to outmaneuver the hardware and the software, and she could only move so fast.

Then again, Angus, he just might be able to accomplish such a herculean effort.

"I'll look into it."

She looked back at Kou. "Looks like we have a potential plan."

"Now we just need to get rid of the prisoners."

The tech frowned down at the indicator on the room's wall display, curiosity getting the better of him. "What's that?" He was only here to do some standard maintenance on relays in Diehli's central monitoring lab, but he'd always had a limitless thirst for knowledge.

A woman looked up, squinting at the screen. "Um, looks like one of our ships has failed to report in."

"Which one?"

She grunted under her breath. "Hold on."

He leaned over her shoulder, looking down at her screen. It wasn't anything he was accustomed to seeing. He spent most of his time repairing systems in the communications room or updating hardware. Still, he was curious. He always had been. This was the whole purpose of his job. If he didn't do it properly, these people wouldn't be able to keep all their ships and personnel in the field safe.

Not a bad day's work, eh?

"Looks like it was an uh… acquisitions ship." Her finger ran down the record on screen. "Most recent mission… acquire some new transportation technology. Neat. Doesn't say what it is, though."

"Why wouldn't they be responding?"

She shook her head. "Any number of reasons. Could be lack of signal, something blocking it."

"Isn't that bad?"

"Maybe, maybe not. There are a lot of natural electromagnetic disturbances that can throw things off, and that doesn't even include governments that don't allow unauthorized ships in certain areas. Forces our guys to turn their ships on stealth mode."

"That happens a lot?"

"More than you would think. But I don't think that's the problem here." She continued scrolling on the screen. Now, it looked like some kind of log. "According to this, they were intercepting their target in an unoccupied system. Should have been easy." She looked up, bringing up a map of the system in question. "I don't see any elements that could negatively impact transmissions here. I'm going to call this in." She looked over her shoulder at him and smiled. "Let's bring our boys home."

CHAPTER FIFTEEN

*S*urg sat in Cass's cargo bay again. This time, Victoria was there. They'd finally managed to pull her away from her research. He'd stood back and waited as she'd slowly and meticulously locked away each item, strong locks clanking into place, then moving onto securing all her data. Curious, he'd watched over her shoulder as she'd engaged encryptions on her devices. His proximity had earned him a glare, which had made him smile. It was good seeing her engaging with him, even if she was annoyed. It was progress.

"Okay, everyone. Thanks for coming," Cass said, clapping her hands together. The sound echoed in the large, open space. He still found it hard to believe this was the same room as Victoria's lab. "Here's the plan we've come up with so far. We can tweak it if needed. Surg, you're going to reach out to your people. Get a team to meet us at a rendezvous point. Angus is going to try to wipe all records of Victoria's existence and research from their databanks. We don't believe any of the people directly after her know anything about what they were hunting, so it should be safe."

Surg leaned forward, pressing his hands into his thighs. "That might be true, but obviously someone *does* know about it. What about them?"

Cass paused, frowning. "I don't know." She shook her head, looking at a loss. She looked over at Victoria, almost like she was apologizing.

"We could implant records that the experiments were nonviable. No point in coming after me if the hypothesis is a dud, right?" Victoria chipped in.

"That could work." Surg nodded.

"Okay, good. We separate the ships, use Angus's control over the Diehli ship to knock out our prisoners and hack the Diehli computers, and we all meet at the rendezvous point. Agreed?"

"Agreed," they all said.

With any likelihood, it was nothing.

The commander stood back from the controls, watching as his team worked, their black uniforms in contrast to the lighter shades of the metal interior. It was a beautiful ship, top of the line. Nothing but the best for him. He'd worked hard for his lot in life, and he deserved it.

Still, it came with obligations, and their current mission was one of them. They'd been ordered to investigate a communications blackout of a ship under Diehli control. It was probably nothing. It happened all the time. Sometimes, the team in question wouldn't even realize they'd lost comms. But then again, sometimes it was far worse. Sometimes, he and his team would arrive to find the crew dead or the ship in a thousand pieces across space, just floating there, so much debris in a vast nothingness.

It could be either, so there was really no point in hypothesizing. The situation would present itself as it would, nothing he could do to change that.

"Sir, I just got something."

He turned to the comms officer to his left. He was turned in his seat at his station, sitting tall and proud. They'd arrived in the sector where they'd last received contact from their ship. "What is it?"

"Not sure. It's definitely on our bandwidths, but it's a strange signal."

"Strange how?" He stepped forward with several quick, long strides and leaned over the other man's shoulder.

"It's too... fast. I don't know." He shook his head, turning back around to face his screen. He pulled up the signal in question, tapping the screen for emphasis. "I can't intercept it, so I don't know its nature, but based on these readings, it's definitely not a normal signal." He paused. "I think it's a cyberhack."

That was bad. Cyberhacks, usually perpetrated by AIs, were computer-originated hacks. They were often more successful than organic hackers because they had a greater flexibility of approach, increased processing power, and drastically reduced response times. Without having to rely on flesh or pre-programmed code, they could infiltrate some of the most secure systems in the universe.

He nodded, his face settling into stern lines. "Send a message to headquarters. They need to be aware of a potential breach."

"Yes, sir."

Victoria didn't know what to think about Surg continuing to stay on the *Discovery*. When they'd made plans for separating the ships, she'd been tempted to ask Cass to take him with her, but that was just stupid. There were only two bedrooms on the *Trojan*, and they were already occupied. It was just practical to allow Surg to remain with her.

It didn't mean she was happy about it. She tended to hesitate when he was in the room with her, like she no longer knew how to react to him, like she no longer knew what he would do. She supposed you never knew what *anyone* would do, but it still left her uncertain and on edge.

Victoria sat in the cockpit, drumming her fingers on the armrest. Their projected path and destination lit up the screen before her. She traced the path with her finger, imagining the various ways their ships could take that path. They could use the sub-space engines, take the ultimate shortcut, which was generally her preference. Or they could use the NauTak drives she'd installed a while back. Slower than sub-space, but drastically faster than the ion propulsion engines she'd installed when the ships were brand new. Those engines were nice in their fuel economy, but unfortunate in being the slowest of the three technologies. Still, it had its uses, like approaching for docking or landing and traveling through debris or asteroid fields.

With a sigh, she dropped her hand. She didn't need to be here, but didn't really want to be anywhere else. She supposed, under normal circumstances, she would have dived into her research once more, maybe working on her prototypes, but that wouldn't solve her problems, and she knew it. How could she fix things if she never faced them head on?

Unfortunately, she'd never been very good at *facing* anything head on. She didn't like conflict, didn't like confrontation, and would avoid it like the plague. That was the hard part. If you never confronted your problems, never did that introspection to figure out what they truly were, you couldn't fix them. But what did she need to fix? She had no doubts there was something, maybe a lot of somethings. She could see it, clear as day, cropping up in her interactions with Cass and Surg. It was like something under pressure. The pressure built too much, and it had to vent. But what was the cause of the pressure, what was the problem, the flaw? Was it her fears? Did she need to conquer them? Or did she need to give Surg a chance? Or maybe she just needed to walk away? Maybe he wasn't the right person for her right now.

There were too many options.

And no amount of logic would point her in the right direction.

I hate this.

This social bullshit was too ephemeral, too intangible. She could learn facial expressions, body language, but nothing translated from one person to the next. Every person was different, and no strategy worked universally. When trying to navigate social problems like this one, she could find herself becoming buried in the choices, the cause and effect. It was too much, too many scenarios. Her brain simply couldn't keep up with all the possible permutations, and that was *if* she could even postulate what effects would happen in each situation.

Victoria leaned back, rubbing her forehead. "Too much." She shook her head, took even breaths, nice and slow. "Surg said to give him a chance." Was she being unfair? "He owns a business. That doesn't necessarily make him a bad person." He hadn't done anything untoward to her so far. He'd helped her with no promise of reward. But did that make him a good person? For that matter, what *did* make a good person?

Feeling a need to escape as tension ramped up within her, Victoria stood and left the cockpit, but didn't know where she wanted to go. She just needed to move. Without conscious thought, her fingers trailed against the metal wall, the cool, smooth sensation pulling her out of her head a bit. At her bedroom door, she hesitated, staring off toward her lab at the end of the hall. She could practically *feel* Surg's room to her right. But was he there?

Anxiety hit her at the thought of encountering him, and her decision was made. She barreled through her bedroom door, slamming it shut behind her.

What is wrong with me?

She took another deep breath.

"Okay. Everything's gonna be okay. Just give it time."

The ship was in sight. The commander stood at attention, staring off into the distance as his crew worked. Fabric shifted against fabric, chairs creaked, and control consoles made their little sounds, signaling each action taken.

At a glance, there seemed to be nothing wrong with the other ship. It was haloed by a large celestial body, big and ominous, though he couldn't tell if it was a planet or asteroid from here. Not that it really mattered what it was. It didn't affect the mission.

He was broken out of his inspection of the ship's image by his signals officer. "I've picked up on two ships preparing to flee, sir."

He frowned, his body immediately tensing, ready for action. Still, he resisted that automatic response, a holdover from his early days with the Diehli. Sometimes, he missed those days.

The action, the adrenaline. There was something energizing about rushing forward in full tactical gear, rifle propped against his shoulder, breathless at the thought of engagement with hostiles. But now, he was a leader. He ran a ship. He had responsibilities, and those two unknown ships presented quite the complication.

A moment later, an image of the ships in question was brought up on screen. They looked identical, though unlike any ship design he'd ever seen. He didn't recognize the model, and he thought he'd learned them all. It helped in his line of work if you knew the ins and outs of every ship you might have to board. But this one was unknown to him.

Interesting.

But he didn't have time now to satisfy his curiosity. They had to act. Time was now of the essence. "Send shuttles after the two fleeing vessels. Our ship will dock with the Diehli ship and check it out."

Surg waited at the door of his bedroom, listening as Victoria's footsteps rushed into her own room. The door slammed shut, and he sighed, reaching for the handle to leave. The hallway was quiet and empty, and he stared for a moment at her door, wanting to be with her but knowing he shouldn't disturb her. He knew she'd been hesitant to take him back on her ship. Knowing that, it was his duty to prove to her she'd made the right decision. He didn't want her to regret it.

He stepped out, careful to be quiet as he turned left and moved to the cockpit. "Angus, I have some calls to make." He sat down.

"Of course."

Surg leaned forward, entering the appropriate communications protocols for contacting his headquarters.

Someone answered almost immediately, though it wasn't who he'd expected. "Where the fuck are you, Surg?"

He was surprised to see his brother's face. "Why are you there?"

"You disappeared? What the beffa did you expect?"

He sighed, suddenly feeling tired. For the first time that he could remember, the gulf between them felt too far to bridge. "I'm fine. I *do* need to organize a team, though."

Varn scowled at him, crossing his arms. His brother had always been the more serious of the two of them. "Your ship was found abandoned on some void-forsaken rock. You never reported in."

"I'm reporting in now." He shrugged, trying to take his brother's aggression in stride. They'd had their share of fights in the past. What two brothers didn't? At some point, the nature of those fights had changed, though. When Varn was younger, he was all rebellion and attitude, while Surg was the calm, responsible one. He'd thought Varn had lost the attitude, though, transitioning from a hormone-ridden boy to a calm, organized businessman, savvy and capable. Meanwhile, Surg had changed from that calm, responsible, ambitious young adult, bent on dragging them out of poverty, to a listless man, suddenly looking around and wondering what he'd built.

"Beffa, Surg. Do you really think this is acceptable?"

He supposed not, but he also knew his brother. He could be intractable, a good thing in business when he saw something he wanted, but less than ideal in relationships. Better to cut this conversation short. "That is neither here nor there. As I said, I need to organize a team. We're going after the Diehli. Any questions?'"

Victoria paced her bedroom, her right hand patting her thigh rhythmically, her thoughts in chaos. Her surroundings were little more than vague impressions and obstacles as she wore a path in her floor. She wanted to believe in Surg. She'd never been so comfortable with a person before. But could she? Could she trust that he had no malicious intents? Could she trust that the siren's song of profit wouldn't drive him to betray her someday?

She wasn't an idiot or blind. Victoria knew what her discovery could mean, even financially. She knew that a person could make a lot of money off instantaneous transportation. She also knew that without proper facilities and resources, it would never be much more than an idea. Without a partner, she would never see her idea take off.

Unfortunately, she'd seen all too readily how a noble idea could be twisted into something dangerous and toxic. She'd seen how a company could abuse the very people they relied on, all for the sake of profit.

But there had to be a middle ground. She just didn't know what it was. If she were a different person, maybe she would have gone into business for herself. She could have run a company building ships or ship parts. But she didn't have what it took to be a businesswoman. She couldn't even imagine what it would take to see such a business to success. She built things, designed things. And she pretty much sucked at everything else.

"A shuttle is approaching," Angus said, disturbing her thoughts.

"What?" she said, jerking to a stop.

"There is a shuttle approaching. I'm recording information on it, but it has failed to respond to comms. I would advise switching to sub-space to lose them."

Her breath froze in her throat.

Not again.

CHAPTER SIXTEEN

*V*ictoria ran to the cockpit, her heart in her throat. It didn't even faze her when she entered to find Surg sitting at the console. "What do we do, Angus?" Her breaths sawed in and out, making her voice thready and weak.

"We've entered sub-space. No sign of the shuttle."

She let out a sigh of relief and sagged against an armrest. "What does this mean? Where are we with the plan?"

"I was in the process of accessing Diehli systems when the shuttle approached."

"Meaning you didn't finish. They still know about us."

"That's correct."

She rubbed her upper chest, trying to think, but this really wasn't her forte. She could rebuild an interstellar engine from the ground up, but ask her to deal with confrontation and her mind went blank.

"I was able to reach out to my company," Surg said, drawing her out of her thoughts before they started spiraling out of control. "A team will be at the rendezvous point."

"That's good." Even to herself, she sounded distracted.

"Angus, can you safely connect with Cass's ship?" Surg said, leaning forward in his seat.

"Aye. One moment."

The screen lit up with a comm window, "Call Connecting," flashing repeatedly.

"Shit," Cass said as the video popped up on screen. Her friend was frowning, looking like she was ready to harm someone.

"Cass?" Victoria said.

Cass jerked her head to look at the camera. "Fuck, Vicky. What the fuck was that?"

"Angus said there was a shuttle approaching. Angus, do you have anything else?"

She waited, hoping, but she was afraid her hope was unfounded. She felt like they were right back where they started, only they didn't have a plan this time.

"I'm analyzing the data I could attain from the shuttle. It was a short range shuttle, which means there was likely a ship nearby," Angus said.

"Damn." Cass looked away from the comm, her face contorted in frustration.

"Also, registration of the shuttle returns to the Diehli."

"Double damn. Well, we can't lead them to the rendezvous site. Angus, is there any way they can track us?"

"Unlikely, but not outside the realm of possibility."

It was a bit weird, hearing Angus's voice coming through the comm. While on her ship, it was easy to think of Angus as a single entity, exclusive to the *Discovery*, like her own private companion. But he was just a program, a program installed in all her ships. There were little differences due to machine learning, but mostly they were identical.

"We'll just have to risk it." Surg sounded very confident in that moment, like he had everything under control.

She looked over at him, watching the way he sat there, tall and steady. His face was calm and relaxed.

Could she trust in that?

The two ships blinked out of existence, completely gone from their sensors. "What the…?" The commander stepped forward. "What just happened?"

"I'm not sure, sir. Looking into it now." The man leaned over his console, his head weaving from side to side as he scanned information. "Our target is human. Most likely, their inter-stellar travel is based on a system using something called sub-space, according to this translation. A byproduct of the system is falling out of what they call 'regular space.' "

"What the hell does that mean?"

He turned around to face his superior. "It means we won't be able to follow them until they stop using their sub-space engines."

"Then we need information. We need to know where they're going. Call back the shuttles."

Surg stood outside Victoria's door with two plates of food. The dishes were warm, the scents taunting his nostrils as he built up the courage to proceed.

This is a dumb idea. I should leave her alone.

But Victoria had barely left her room since they'd entered sub-space, and he knew she hadn't eaten anything. She should be hungry, right? She had to eat.

Right?

"Angus, can you let Victoria know I'm here with food?"

"Of course."

Moments passed. Did Angus tell her? Did she refuse? He assumed she hadn't, or surely Angus would have informed him. He looked back toward the kitchen. Maybe this was a terrible idea.

He snorted at himself. He hadn't felt this uncertain of himself since he was a dirt broke near-adult with no parents.

The door slipped open, exposing a sliver of Victoria's face.

"Hi." He lifted the two plates. "I brought food."

Looking down at his offerings, she smiled. "Come on in." She stepped back, hand still on the door handle. "There's a table in the corner."

He turned in the direction she'd indicated. To the right, a small table and chairs took up one corner of the room. It was covered in what looked like a sweater, a book, some hopefully clean dishes, and a stuffed animal.

"Yeah, sorry." She walked ahead of him. The sweater got thrown on the back of a chair. She threw the book and a bright purple stuffed animal on the bed, then rushed the dishes off to a sink he could see through a doorway next to the table.

Surg set the two plates down on the freshly cleared surface, and Victoria came back, looking embarrassed.

"Hey, it's your room." He rested his hands on the back of the chair in front of him. The material was cold, but he didn't think it was metal. "Let's eat."

She nodded. "Yes, let's." She sat down across from him, looking as skittish as a wild animal in a city. Looking down at her food, she took little bites, shoveling each bit slowly with her utensil.

After a few minutes, she held the empty utensil in midair. Her words seemed to come out of nowhere. "I don't know what to think. I know that..." She let out a slow breath, lowering the utensil to the plate with a clatter. "Before I knew it, I was comfortable with you. I was comfortable to an extent I'm not sure I've ever been. I can't explain it. I don't know how to."

Surg held his breath, hope rising to choke him, save him, or crush him. She was talking to him. She was saying nice things. He kept quiet, hoping to hear more, knowing any words from him would shut her up, possibly for good.

"But I don't know how to trust you. You're not the person I thought you were."

He wanted to object, to tell her he was, but he couldn't. It wouldn't help his cause. It would probably just drive her away.

She ran a finger along the edge of her plate, still not looking at him. "When I met you, you were covered in dust. You saved my life. I can't thank you enough. I guess I just assumed. I jumped to conclusions I had no evidence to back. You could have been anyone. I mean, even *I* was covered in dust that day. Your appearance didn't really tell me anything about you, but like I said, I assumed.

"And you've never given me reason to think you were a businessman, certainly not one as significant as that." She paused, her focus seeming to shift completely to the movement of her fingers before continuing with a sigh. "I'm sorry. I don't know how to do this. My past has told me not to trust you. I want to. I do. But how? How do I get over this?"

He reached out, hovering his hand near hers. She didn't pull away, so he rested his hand over hers for comfort. Her fingers were cold, and he rubbed them, warming them. "With time. With experience. All you need is to be patient. I get you were hurt, but I don't want to hurt you. I've tried everything I can not to hurt you."

He continued to rub her hand, watching her face and body language for tells. "Before you, I was lonely. I had an empire, so to speak, but I had no one. Even my own brother is distant." He shook his head. "I don't know what happened to us. We used to be inseparable. I did this for us, built that company for us, but now I hardly ever see him.

"Checking up on that lead was a way for me to get out of the office, to get away for a bit. I could have sent the team I'd organized, but I didn't. I figured it was a long shot and didn't want to waste their time." He chuckled. "Long shot, indeed."

Finally, she looked up at him, a small smile on her face. "Yeah, you found me."

"That, I did."

That… I did.

"Status?" the commander said as he waited on his ship.

"The airlock doors are intact," a member of the breach team said through comms. "But oxygen levels are subpar. We'll need to wear breathing apparati when we go in."

The commander watched the large screen, where tactical cameras showed what his team saw. Right now, they were still at their own airlock. They'd connected with the other ship, the two airlocks sealed together. Some views showed the backs of black uniforms.

"Let's move." The video jerked as the team went into motion. The hissing of their breathers came over the comms. Otherwise, silence reigned as they waited for the airlocks to do their jobs and the mission to really begin. Once the doors opened, they stormed through, a cacophony of shaking visuals even their image stabilizers couldn't completely compensate for.

In spite of that, the team did proceed with caution, waiting at every corner, checking that it was safe. They didn't want to step into an ambush unaware. One screen dipped, exposing a portable computer. "Sensors don't indicate any explosive ordinance."

A blur of movement caught the corner of his eye as the team leader motioned them forward. They moved through the ship with efficiency. "Checking the computer systems."

"Fuck, this is a mess," the computer specialist said through the comms. "What did they do to this thing?"

The team stood in the command center of the ship. From the commander's position, everything seemed in order. The surfaces were clean. None of the panels were open or damaged. What was the problem?

Pointing to the computer guy, the team lead said, "You stay here. Fix this mess. The rest of us, let's go find us some survivors."

The video feeds split. "Follow me. We've got heat signatures in this direction." The team lead was looking down at a heat overlay map.

The commander held his breath, praying this would not be another mission where they brought back nothing but dead bodies. He could do it. That was his job. But that didn't mean he had to like it.

"Found two survivors."

The commander jerked his head up. The team was in a room with two people unconscious on the floor. "Status?"

"Alive. Probably knocked out by low oxygen levels." The team lead pointed at several members of his team. "You four, take these guys back to medical. The rest of you, let's search the rest of the ship. I don't want any surprises."

Again, the video streams split. The commander pressed a button to open comms with medical. "I need medics with two stretchers at the airlock."

"Yes, sir," came over the comm.

Though he couldn't be seen, he nodded anyway, and switched back to the comm with the infiltrating team. On video, the team moved silently through the ship. Each room was searched with two men sweeping the room while the team lead watched their backs from the hall, making sure no one snuck up on them.

His mind drifted to the men on their way to medical while the team checked room after empty room. Would they be okay? What had been done to them? The video hadn't given him a good look at the men, so he didn't know what type of shape they were in. Hopefully, it was only hypoxia, nothing more. If so, they would snap out of it as soon as the oxygen levels increased.

That would be the best-case scenario.

On screen, the search finished. The team returned to check on the computer specialist. When they entered, he was still situated on the floor, his computer in his lap.

"What's the status?" the team lead said as he entered.

The specialist tilted his head up. "Not great. These systems are heavily compromised. Based on this level of damage, I'd say an AI was involved. Every single system has been affected."

"Can we get this thing limping along? Can we get it back to headquarters?"

He shook his head. "Not until we work some of this out. Whoever did this didn't want this ship to move any time soon. Navigation and propulsion controls are both shot. I've already fixed life support. All they did there was drop the air output. They were pretty precise about it." He looked up at the team lead. "I don't think they had any intention of killing. I think the point was to get a head start."

The team lead nodded.

"Can we find out where they're going?" the commander interrupted over comms.

The specialist shrugged. "Maybe. Depends. I can try to pull up surveillance data. I have a couple programs that should be able to scan data to find useful information, but first, I have to unwind this mess. Surveillance was one of the systems that was compromised."

"ETA?" the commander asked.

"Maybe fifteen diceros? Not long."

The commander nodded and leaned back, looking over the command center of his ship, where much of his crew waited for his next order, eager to begin the chase. "Get to it."

"Yes, sir."

Victoria dropped into bed fully clothed later that day. She grunted when she landed on the book from earlier. She dug it out from under her and tossed it to the floor. More comfortable, she sighed and relaxed into the soft bedding.

Except she couldn't quite relax. How could she? There were still people after her, and she still hadn't come to any conclusions about Surg. On one level, she just wanted it all to be over. She wanted to just be done with it, for things to be back to normal, but she didn't think that would make her any happier. It would just reduce her stress levels.

"I'm a mess," she said as her hand touched on the other thing she'd thrown on her bed earlier, the stuffed animal. It was a unicorn and soft as a cloud. She'd always liked stuffed animals. As a girl, she'd had so many they'd covered her bed. She couldn't lay down in it without disrupting them.

Now, when she was stressed or felt fractured, petting a stuffed animal kept her together, kept her a little more sane. Today, was no different. She stared up at the ceiling as she absently ran her fingers over the unicorn's silky fur.

The conversation with Surg earlier had gone really well. She still didn't know what to do, didn't know how to trust him, but it had helped her remember why she'd let him get close in the first place.

She remembered the moment when he'd hesitated to touch her hand, waiting to see how she would react. Looking back, she could remember countless examples of the very same behavior. He always seemed to know when to give her space, always seemed to perfectly gage what she needed. Even her best friends rarely pulled it off well. Just take the moment in the galley when Cass had pushed her so hard, she'd run off back to her room. She'd felt cornered, trapped, and Cass just hadn't been able to see it. Why couldn't she see it? How could she not know?

She couldn't understand why people couldn't just pay attention. Was it so hard to see when you were pushing someone too far? Was it so hard to pull yourself out of your own head long enough to be aware?

Victoria was socially inept, but she'd never had a problem with that element. In fact, she remembered this autistic kid she knew growing up. He'd been older than her by years, but he was considered "low functioning." At least, that's what his parents called him. He'd always seemed very happy as long as people listened to him, paid attention. He was often sensory seeking, but didn't like being hugged or interacting with people. Still, she'd always seen him as misunderstood, not broken. He would play loud music, loved bright colors, and eventually got a job he loved. When people left him to his own devices, he was happy. When people gave him clear instructions, he excelled.

She'd envied him.

People in her life had never paid attention, never left her to her own devices. She'd "excelled," but it had taken a hefty toll, one she hadn't wanted to pay. To her, it sometimes felt like the entire world was attacking her, even when she didn't really notice. Sometimes, she couldn't even say what was wrong. The best way she could describe it was like claustrophobia, like everything was boxing her in from all sides.

Except she didn't fear small spaces. And she could experience it in large rooms. It wasn't the size of the room that was the problem. She just couldn't put words to what she was feeling.

As her thoughts spiraled out of control, her gaze mapped the ceiling and her fingers desperately ran repetitive patterns over the toy in her arms.

Why am I dwelling on this yet again?

It wasn't the time or place. There were people out to get her, for Christ's sake. She needed a plan. She needed to get her head on straight. Even focusing on her relationship with Surg was a waste of time at the moment. She had bigger problems to deal with, namely, the Diehli.

Right now, the plan was to rendezvous with the *Trojan* and the team Surg had gathered, but what if that shuttle followed them to their destination? Could they? Could they set up an ambush?

She knew the shuttle had to belong to a larger ship. That ship had found them once. She had to believe they would find them again. She had to operate under that assumption.

So, what could they do? How could they mitigate the risk?

Come on, Victoria. Think.

She was smart, wicked smart. And she knew spaceships better than pretty much anybody. She'd spent her life staring at schematics, technical manuals, and parts. She might not know squat about tactics and combat, but she knew ships.

And knowing the territory was half the battle, right?

"Sir? Analysis is complete," the computer specialist said through the comm.

"Report." The commander had taken to sitting at his console as he waited, going over updates and communiques. He stood from his seat, eager for information.

"It'll take time to get the ship's systems up and running again. My advice is to call in a maintenance team for the job. Meanwhile, I was able to access surveillance data on the ship. There are a few things I was able to glean from that data."

"Yes?" the commander said, a little impatient with the conversation. Around him, the rest of the crew had surreptitiously started listening in, all their forms just a little too still as they angled themselves toward the screen.

The specialist sucked in a breath, sitting up straighter. "We know the crew was interrogated. One of the interrogators was Inia Surg, sir. He was specifically mentioned at one point during the boarding."

"Void be damned," the commander said, looking away. Of all the people to get involved in the situation, that self-righteous prick, incapable of keeping his nose out of other people's businesses, was the last person he wanted to hear mentioned. He'd been on more than a few operations where Inia Intergalactic had interfered, and it always made things more complicated than he liked.

Admittedly, more than a few of those operations had contained objectives to steal from Inia Intergalactic itself, but that was beside the point. The bastard had no business interfering this time, and the man should mind his own business.

"What else?"

"I confirmed there was an AI involved. I believe its designation is 'Angus.' Not that I know what that means." He shrugged. "We can confirm from our surveillance that our scientist, Victoria Chan, *was* there. For a bulk of the time, the

Diehli ship was attached to two other ships, so it sounds like she had help.

"And best yet? I was able to catch audio from the other ships. It was faint and required a lot of creative programming to pull a transcript, but I know where they're going."

CHAPTER SEVENTEEN

*V*ictoria sat in the cockpit, waiting. They were almost to their destination, and soon they would be leaving sub-space. She always loved watching that. It was probably her favorite part of being in space.

"Leaving sub-space," Angus said in warning.

Victoria gripped her armrests, anticipation energizing her body. She wanted to move, but wouldn't miss this for the world. The universe through the viewscreen blended into a kaleidoscopic swirl of colors, stretching like taffy being made, then fell away, leaving just as beautiful a scene. The ship was surrounded by near-endless black.

They were far and away from anything and everything. They'd wanted it that way. After all, you wanted cover when you were setting up an ambush. You wanted wide open spaces when you were on defense.

And they were definitely on defense now. "Surg, we're here," she yelled behind her, her voice echoing down the hallway.

Surg's head peeked out of his room. "Are the others here yet?"

"Aye," Angus said overhead. "They were waiting for us to arrive."

Surg stepped into the hall, the door closing behind him with a click. "Good. We need to talk."

Yes, they did. Their plan had already fallen through. Angus hadn't finished his hack of Diehli systems, which meant they still knew about her. What was worse, there was a possibility the other ship would find them. She didn't know how. She'd only seen the shuttle, so she didn't know what type of ship it docked with. Did any species have technology that could track movement through sub-space? She wasn't sure. She knew a lot of alien tech, probably more than most. Reading white papers and technical manuals was her favorite way of winding down before bed. But still, some technology just wasn't public knowledge, and she wasn't a hacker like Cass. Trade secrets and military tech were outside her reach, and Diehli seemed like the type to keep their favorite tech to themselves. She wouldn't put it past them to have a few tricks up their sleeves.

In truth, they reminded her of the old days, back when she was a teenager, back before she'd moved to the caravan. There was a similar aggression to the Diehli's approach, a ruthless determination that said, "I'll get what I want. It's only a matter of time." It was that drive, that unrelenting push for more, more, more that had sent her flying right past her breaking point. She refused to let it happen again.

Surg sat down next to her. "Angus, call the other ships."

"Aye, sir."

The view changed from the unrelenting black of space to two video screens. They waited for the calls to connect.

The *Trojan* connected first. "Fuck, you guys are okay. Thank Christ." Cass leaned back in her chair, looking a little worse for wear. Frantic color covered her face, and strands of her short purple hair were sticking straight up.

"We're fine," Surg said, leaning forward with his elbows on his thighs. "Although we definitely had a bit of a scare."

"A shuttle, right?" Cass asked.

"Yup. Came out of nowhere."

The other screen popped up, showing a striking woman with stern features and a buzz cut. She sat tall, the black collar of her shirt pristine.

"Taln," Surg said, nodding in greeting. "Everyone, this is Taln. She'll be running the team I organized from Inia Intergalactic. Taln, the woman next to me is Victoria. On the other screen, you have Cass, Kou, and Jessie." He pointed to each, they waved when he said their names.

Taln nodded, but didn't speak.

"As we were saying before you connected, the plans are probably going to have to change. We weren't able to hack Diehli systems, and there was another ship there when we left. That was what precipitated our departure. We know there were two short range shuttles in the area, which means there was a larger ship nearby."

"Two shuttles?" Taln asked, her expression not changing.

"Yes."

She nodded. "That means it's a fairly large ship. Probably a large crew." Taln turned her head to the side. "I want you to get me a list of ship classes that could handle two shuttles. Cross reference it against known ships the Diehli owns or contracts with."

"Yes, sir," a disembodied voice said over the comm.

Taln turned back to the camera. "Do you think you were followed?"

"Not likely," Victoria said. *At least, I hope not.* "We dropped into sub-space."

Taln nodded thoughtfully. "Proprietary human technology. I don't know of any other species that use it. But we can check and see if there are any known tracking systems that work across those spaces. There's not any chance they still have tracking on you, right?"

Surg scoffed. "I would hope not. We've scoured this ship from top to bottom."

Victoria looked at him funny. "No, we haven't. It would take years to 'scour this ship from top to bottom.' " She looked at Taln. "We have done a thorough search, though. We've focused mainly on finding alien software because any system that didn't use native hardware would be easy to find. It would be too big unless it had a very small effective transmission distance."

Taln nodded again. "Which would be useless. Good. So, it's highly unlikely they could have followed you here."

"But not impossible, right?" Kou said over Cass's shoulder.

"No, not impossible." Taln sat straighter as she caught sight of Kou, who was the embodiment of a soldier for his people. His was a startling visage, with half his exposed body covered in metal from past injuries in combat and a single electric blue eye playing counterpart to his natural black one. "We'll have to take that into account with our planning, but it's an unlikely scenario at this point in time."

"So, what are we going to do now? Our original plan is moot at this point. Without the other ship, it's possible Angus can't hack into Diehli. The ship served as a back door."

Victoria looked over at Surg as he spoke. He was tense, but she wasn't sure that would be visible over comms. He kept himself poised, his body language speaking of authority. How did he do that?

"Okay, I'll get back to you as soon as I have more information," Taln said, jerking Victoria out of her thoughts. The other woman smiled, a cocky grin that looked almost sinister. "Don't worry. This is what I do."

The commander sat in his chair, staring out at nothingness. He'd commanded his people to fly them close to the coordinates they'd discovered, but far enough away that they couldn't be discovered on long range scans.

"Tell me if anything changes." He pushed himself to his feet, leaving the control room.

"Yes, sir," a chorus of voices said to his back as he traversed the hallway.

The space was dark and empty, even though it was lit. Everyone was at their stations, leaving no one to idly wander. Halfway down the hall, he pressed his hand to a panel that caused the door beside it to slide open. "Tell me our status," he said as he entered.

The team leader sat up taller at the conference table. His team sat around him, each of them in various poses, none of them what he would call sitting. "We believe the shuttles will be capable of operating in stealth so long as there are no organic eyes watching.

"Which means striking while they're sleeping."

"And how are we supposed to know when they're sleeping?"

The team leader stood, his hands clasped behind his back. "Well, we're in luck. I reviewed the camera footage and surveillance data. From that, we were able to determine what part of their wake-sleep cycle they were in. And based on known biology, we're able to estimate a standard circadian cycle for humans. We can extrapolate on that as to when the middle of their next rest cycle will be."

"Excellent. How long?"

He pulled up something on his computer, showing the screen to his commanding officer.

A timer filled the display, counting down to mission start.

Surg yawned as he woke, stretching in bed. For a room that was never used, the bed was surprisingly comfortable. Pushing back the sheets, he dropped his legs over the side of the bed and shivered as bare skin hit the cold floor. "Ugh." He rubbed his face, trying to wake up.

His morning routine felt slow, his body moving sluggishly through space and time. His brain might as well have still been back in that bed for all the good it did him.

Though I'd much rather be in another bed.

Surg stopped, imagining waking up next to Victoria. He smiled. She would be in his arms, her warm body pressed to his. Or maybe her hair would be tickling his face, making him want to brush it aside, but hesitant to do so in fear of waking her. Or maybe he would wake up with a pervasive chill because she'd hogged the blankets, and he would get up carefully, leaving her to her blanket nest.

God, I'm hopeless.

Because all of that sounded wonderful.

"Just patience, Surg. She'll come around." He got dressed and tried to focus on the task at hand... keeping Victoria safe. Right now, his feelings were just a distraction. If they didn't get the Diehli off her ass, he would *never* have a chance with her.

He stepped into the hallway and stared at Victoria's closed door. It was always closed, but in that moment, it felt almost symbolic.

Quit it, Surg.

He needed to eat and check in with Taln. Unfortunately, Taln hadn't called since that first contact yesterday. He supposed that was to be expected. Her team had a lot to do. It might take time to go through all the data, to come up with a plan. But that was what he paid her for, and he should let her do her job.

So, instead of heading to the cockpit, he turned right toward the kitchen. He would check with her after breakfast.

In the kitchen, he stared at the display screen, scrolling through options. There were a lot of options, almost all of them human dishes he didn't recognize. The entire display was in a human language he couldn't read. He supposed it made sense. The system was designed with humans in mind. While Angus might have to interact with members of other species, there was no reason to think an alien would need to use the kitchen. So far, he'd repeated the same few meals, using symbology he'd memorized from when Victoria had chosen food for him.

He sighed, picking something at random.

The robot whirred into action. He didn't recognize many of the ingredients, though it did seem there were some items he *did* recognize.

Probably substitutions. How long has it been since Victoria returned to Earth?

Did she ever return home? Did she even *think* of it as home anymore? Surg got the feeling she was running from something. She'd admitted to some things with him, but was there more? What was *truly* driving her?

The plate clinked as it settled on the deck, and he picked it up, staring down at the offerings. Some things were obvious, like an intact fruit, though he didn't know what the fruit was called. There were also a couple slices of bread, though they looked different from when it had been used as a sandwich in a previous meal. Browner, crisper. Other than that, there was something fluffy and yellow and something thin, crispy, and greasy.

He popped one of the greasy strips into his mouth. "Hmm, not bad." He suspected he'd eaten it before. It reminded him of something from the sandwich he'd had.

His mind returned to the task at hand as he continued to pop food into his mouth and chew. He should talk with Taln next, check on her status. Hopefully, she'd made progress by now.

Finishing his food, he washed his dishes and turned his back on the kitchen, moving to the cockpit. He dropped into the left seat. "Connect me with the *Areon*, please."

Angus didn't respond, and he looked up at the speaker, wondering if the AI was upset with him. He leaned forward and tapped the screen. It only took a couple selections to redial the *Areon*.

A small screen popped up, and he waited, his stomach uncomfortably full from the large breakfast he'd selected.

"Inia, sir," Taln said the moment she popped up on the screen.

"Taln." He nodded in greeting. "Any updates?"

"I have my team working hard. We will let you know as soon as we have something. I won't let you down, sir."

"I know you won't. I only hire the best."

Her face slipped into a rare smile before her stern expression returned. "Yes, sir."

"Well, carry on. I'll check back in soon."

"Yes, sir."

He leaned forward and ended the transmission. Sighing, he sat back in his seat, staring out into space. If he stared long enough, it almost felt like the universe was consuming him, like it was growing to overwhelm him completely.

He looked away, staring back at the empty hallway. Was Victoria up yet? He stood up, leaning toward the door before his feet had even moved. Maybe she was in her lab. He didn't consciously note his footsteps as he traveled to the other end of the ship. At the doorway to the lab, he stopped, surprised to find it empty and quiet, almost tomblike.

He turned back, checking in the kitchen, but it, too, was empty. He spun around. "Angus, is Victoria awake?"

Angus didn't respond.

He waited, his fingers digging into the doorframe at his sides. "Angus? Are you there? Is Victoria awake?"

Still, Angus said nothing, and a sickening dread started to fill him. Before he knew it, he was at Victoria's door, banging hard against the metal. "Victoria! Answer me! Are you okay?"

But silence answered him instead.

Surg tried the handle. He would deal with her wrath later if necessary, but he needed to know she was okay. He didn't understand why Angus was being so unhelpful. The door flew open, exposing an empty room. All her things were still there, the barely contained chaos still in existence, but its source was absent. "Victoria?" he said hesitantly as he stepped into the room, moving toward the bathroom, the only area he couldn't see from the door. "Please tell me you're okay. I'm sorry I came in without permission, but I just need to know you're okay."

The continued quiet was like a heavy presence in the room, speaking testimony to the truth.

He reached the bathroom. It, too, was empty.

Where the hell was she?

CHAPTER EIGHTEEN

*S*urg stood in the cockpit of Victoria's ship. It felt wrong to be there without her, but what choice did he have? After finding her missing, he'd contacted Taln. Her team was investigating, scouring the *Discovery* for any leads.

Next to him, Cass investigated Angus's programming, grumbling and cursing intermittently. They'd figured out early on that Surg's computer specialists couldn't make heads or tails of Angus's programming. Humans were such a small player on the intergalactic scale that most other species hadn't bothered to really familiarize themselves with their preferred programming and technologies.

His gaze alternated between Cass's back and the hallway, where he could see people in black uniforms checking Victoria's bedroom door while more moved in the lab, their intent unclear from his perch.

And I'm doing nothing.

Cass pushed back from her work, drawing his focus.

"Did you find something?"

"Unfortunately, yes." She shook her head. "Fuck, man, this makes no sense. It seems like they didn't know enough about his programming to hack him. Or at least I can't see any evidence of them trying. His code looks sound. And from his records, he was completely disconnected sometime early this morning. But there's nothing, like a switch was flipped and suddenly he was offline. I'm gonna have to check the hardware."

"Well, that would certainly explain why he didn't warn us."

"But it makes no sense." Cass stood, pacing in the small space in front of Surg. "How did they do it? Anything they did should have required access I could track from his databases, but there's nothing. It's like whatever they did shut him down remotely and instantaneously, so fast he didn't even log the event. It makes no sense."

Surg leaned back against the wall, crossing one ankle over the other as he thought. Cass continued to pace in front of him. He understood what Cass was saying. If they'd approached or boarded the ship before disabling Angus, there would be surveillance data to pull. But there was nothing. How was that possible? How could they shut the AI down remotely?

"What do you know about Angus's hardware?"

Cass shook her head. "Not my department. Victoria's the hardware specialist. I mean, I'm gonna take a look, see if there's anything obvious, but no promises."

She chuckled to herself as she moved toward the door with purpose. "I've actually done more than my fair share of main-tenance and tweaks on the *Trojan*. You'd think a new ship wouldn't need it, but these ships are custom. Small production line. There's always something." She looked behind her. "But don't tell Vicky that. She'd probably burst a blood vessel."

Surg followed on her heels. "What can I do to help?" He *needed* something to do. Staying inside his own head, rehashing what he could have done to prevent this, would just drive him mad.

"Probably nothing."

"Oh, Inia, sir." The person kneeling next to Victoria's door stood. "The lock was definitely engaged." He pointed at the door, where scrapes and discolorations in a distinctive pattern marred the surface near the lock mechanism. "See these marks? I've seen them before. It's made with proprietary technology."

"Let me guess. Owned by the Diehli."

"Exactly. Can't count the amount of pirated ships I've seen with these marks on them."

Surg nodded his head and turned as Cass continued forward with a curse under her breath. "Fucking bastards," she said a little louder, her boots stomping on the flooring with hard claps of sound.

"We'll get her back."

Cass spun, pointing a finger into his chest. "You bet your damn ass, we will."

Surg lifted his hands in the air. "Hey, I'm not the enemy."

Cass sighed and turned around, stepping into the lab. "I know you're not." As she wandered aimlessly through the space, she ignored the people roaming around, hunting for clues. "It's just, I've always looked after her. I feel like somehow it's my fault."

"It's not. You weren't even here."

She rounded on him, her purple locks slapping against her face, making him realize she hadn't done anything with them today. They just dangled limply against her head. "That's the problem! I wasn't here!" She ran fingers through her hair. "I should have been here."

He touched her shoulder, holding firm. "No, you shouldn't have. This is no one's fault." He said it, even if he didn't believe it. If anyone was at fault, it was him. *He* was the one who'd been here. *He* was the one who'd failed her. He could have stopped this. He *should* have stopped this. If only he'd been awake. If only he'd heard *something.* How could someone have entered the ship, taken Victoria, and left him none the wiser? Screw Angus. How did *he* not notice anything?!

"I guess it doesn't matter now," Cass said, shrugging off his hand. She nodded her head toward the wall. "Let's go check on the hardware."

"Right."

Cass pressed on one of the wall panels. It clicked and popped outward. She grabbed the edge and pushed is aside, revealing a maintenance hallway.

"Clever." It'd been open the last time he and Victoria had gone in there, so he hadn't seen how it operated.

She looked back and smiled. "That's Victoria for you. Back when she lived with me and my sister, she used to talk about haunted houses, about the ones with the secret passages. It was the only thing that interested her other than spaceships. I think she loved the idea of having somewhere she could retreat, somewhere to hide when she wanted to be alone. I can understand that. Sometimes, I'm not fit for company either."

They stepped into the new hallway, Cass in the lead. Dim lighting turned on automatically as they entered. The guts of the ship were showcased on either side in neat stacks and bundles. Everything was labeled and looked to be in its rightful place.

"I'm going to start with the breakers and electrical system." She shook her head. "I can't think of anything else that could have been done remotely."

He nodded, but Cass didn't see him. She walked on, completely ignoring him and leaving him to his thoughts. He didn't want that, though. His thoughts weren't exactly healthy right now. His mind was a miasma of self-blame and self-doubt, topped with raging feelings of inferiority with no source or escape.

Surg wanted Victoria back. He wanted her here, safe. He wanted to deserve her, but didn't think he could. After all, *he'd* been the one here. *He'd* driven her away by not telling her the whole truth. What right did he have to her attention, her affection?

But it didn't matter anymore. All that mattered was getting her back.

"Oh my fucking God," Cass breathed.

Surg jerked his head in her direction, surprised by the slack jawed look of shock on her face. "What? What is it?"

"You're lucky you're not dead."

"What?" He rushed forward, trying to figure out what she saw that he didn't. To him, it looked much like everything else in this area. "What am I seeing?"

She pointed at an area in front of her. A bunch of labeled switches ran in columns up and down the wall. "This is the main circuit breaker panel of the *Discovery*. It controls power to every major system on the ship."

He stared at it, trying to make sense of the panel, to see if anything was wrong. He knew an issue here could be devastating to a ship, but everything was in a foreign language, one he didn't know. "How bad is it?"

She pointed at one of the switches. "This and all the ones below it control life support. Almost all of them are tripped."

"Tripped?"

"It means there's no power."

"Right." He blanched. "That's very bad."

"Yes." She nodded. "Yes, it is." She moved over several rows. "This one powers Angus's systems. Also tripped. These here power many of the surveillance systems. Not all of them tripped, but with Angus's breaker tripped, it wouldn't matter. It looks random, though, like they threw a bunch of darts at a wall and just happened to hit a few bullseyes."

"Can it be fixed?"

"Sure. This isn't even hard. Just need to push all the breakers to the right."

He stepped up to the wall. "Is there any particular order it needs to be done in?"

"I don't think so. Then again, I don't usually have this many tripped at once."

"Okay. I start from the left, you start from the right?"

"Sure."

He started flipping switches. They were tougher than he expected. Each one required force, and they were too short to get it by leverage.

"Man, you're lucky comms worked."

"What?" He turned to her, his fingers on the next switch.

She kept flipping the switches to the right, one by one. "Well, if the comms breakers had been tripped, you would have died."

"What do you mean?"

"Life support has been offline since the break in. Angus wasn't online to raise an alarm. If you hadn't contacted us, we wouldn't have known something was wrong. Right now, mine and Taln's ships are the only things keeping this ship habitable. Without us, oxygen levels would have eventually dropped until you passed out and died."

Victoria startled awake, immediately knowing something was very wrong. Usually, she either woke feeling like her skin was sore from sleeping too long or like she was lying on a cloud. Today, something hard dug into her upper arm where it stretched out to her side, and she felt like she was sleeping on a camp chair.

She sat up, and her mouth fell open, blind fear stalling her out. Her brain felt like it couldn't quite process what she was seeing, what she was feeling. For a spell, she was just shocked, stuck in a state of "other."

Her hand rose to rub the skin of her chest. She took deep breaths, but each felt just a little shaky. She was holding onto her calm by the tips of her fingers. Her gaze roamed the room, the only sound being her breath sawing in and out of her lungs.

She was in a lab, though one she'd never seen before. Her cot was against one wall, an emergency shower and eye wash station at the head of it, though she didn't recognize the specific design. The rest of the walls held shelves, cabinets, and workstations in uninterrupted lines. Another workstation split the room in two, taking up the middle of the floor-space. The counters were clean and clear, with just a few computer stations breaking up the pristine surface.

Why am I here?

What the hell happened?

"Ah, you're awake." A voice broke into the silence.

Victoria jerked her head up, spotting the intercom speaker and camera in the corner. "What do you want?"

"We are interested in the instantaneous transportation you were developing."

"You mean you want to steal it," she snapped, pushing to her feet, her arms stiff, hands fisted at her sides.

"That's not how I would phrase it, no. We simply wish you to develop the technology for us. You will be rewarded handsomely."

"Bullshit. You don't kidnap people *and* reward them. That's not how the world works."

"Ah, but this isn't your world, is it, human?"

She frowned, her hands twitching at her sides. "I'll admit I'm not as 'worldly' as some, but from what I've seen, some things are universal. And *nobody* is so forgiving that they'd willingly work for you after being kidnapped."

"You're probably right, but where bribes don't work, threats usually do."

"What's that supposed to mean?"

"Let's speak it plainly then. Do what we ask, or we'll kill your friends."

CHAPTER NINETEEN

*V*ictoria paced her prison cell, running her fingers lightly over the neighboring surfaces as she circled the central island. Her hands shook, her breathing was erratic, and she couldn't think. All she could focus on were her friends and Surg. And even then, it was more raw emotion than actual thoughts.

Fear.

Panic.

Victoria wanted to save them. She wanted to get out of here and keep them safe, but she couldn't even get her own brain to cooperate. She was useless, hopeless. *Cass* was the badass one. *Ellie* was the diplomatic one. Victoria just really liked spaceships.

"Gah!" she yelled, her hands flailing at her sides, trying to escape all this toxic energy and tension. She started sobbing in frustration, though no tears fell.

This was all her fault. If she hadn't been so obsessed with ships, she wouldn't be here. She would have never ended up on their radar. Maybe she would have been living a normal life on Earth right now. Her parents never would have pushed her into doing all those design contracts. She never would have been diagnosed with Generalized Anxiety Disorder. She would have never been emancipated. What would she be doing now? Would she have finished high school? Graduated college?

It made her realize she had a very strange life. She'd never graduated high school. Never gone to college. Never had friends in school. She'd become obsessed with spaceships at an early age. She'd only paid attention when her parents read her books about spaceships and space travel. When she could read on her own, she'd always picked books on those same subjects. Later, she'd run out of kids' books and started reading textbooks. She'd started drawing, too.

That was the beginning of the end, really. She'd eventually created a blog where she posted her drawings, her thoughts. It had helped her feel connected when every conversation had either not interested her or ended up one sided. Just the idea that someone might be looking, might be reading, was enough.

As her drawing skills and knowledge grew, she continued to post her ideas. Her earliest postings were little more than childlike drawings. Her later ones were technical drafts, sometimes of entire ships, sometimes of individual parts. She loved paying attention to every detail, looking at other designs and tweaking them, making them better. Sometimes it was about the artistry, sometimes it was about the functionality.

Then one day, she'd received an email. The person had no idea she was only fourteen. They'd seen her blog and had wanted her to work with their design team to fix a flaw in an upcoming product. She'd been so excited. She'd felt valued for the very first time.

A part of her now wished she'd never responded.

Except, then, she would have never met Surg. That thought stopped her in her tracks. Without those series of events, her obsessions, she would have never left Earth, would she? Would she even have her friends? The day she'd met Cass, Jessie, and Ellie, her parents had taken her to the park to get her out of the house, to force her to socialize. If she'd not been so obsessed, they might not have felt that need. They might have never gone to that park.

She fell back against the counter behind her, a hard edge digging into her back. An undefinable emotion rolled around in her gut. She couldn't make sense of her own thoughts, her own emotions. She'd always been the odd one out, on the outskirts of this friendship they all shared. Jessie and Cass were thick as thieves, and while Ellie wasn't always there, she always swooped in and resumed their friendship like she'd only walked away moments ago. Meanwhile, Victoria had always been on the sidelines, either looking on in bafflement at their easy companionship or perfectly content to be left out, doing her own thing.

But Surg was different. If you'd asked her before meeting him, she would have said she didn't want anything more. She would have said she was content, happy, the way things were. But, somehow, Surg gave her just what she needed. Cass could be too pushy, not knowing when to quit. Talking with Ellie was a bit of an adventure, since Victoria didn't always catch her sarcasm. And she never got a dose of Jessie without Cass nearby anymore.

But Surg knew when to push her, knew when to hold back. He moved through their interactions like it was an elegant dance. And like a good dance partner, he led her through effortlessly, even though she wasn't a good dancer herself. He made it easy.

She couldn't let these bastards harm any of them. She needed to think, to plan, to act.

———

Cass paced her bedroom, agitated and irritated that she couldn't do anything. She'd fixed the power issues on the *Discovery*, restored Angus, and confirmed he knew nothing. There was nothing more she could do. Surg's team was working to come up with more information, to come up with a plan.

The problem was, they all knew what had happened. People working for the Diehli had taken Vicky in the middle of the night. No matter where they'd taken her, it wasn't good. If they'd taken her to a satellite location, they might never find her. If they'd taken her to headquarters, they might never get to her. Cass was just a pirate, a privateer now. What did she know about storming a stronghold like Diehli headquarters? Surg had been struggling against the company for years professionally, and he'd never gotten anywhere. What could a single pirate do against *that*?

"Easy," Kou said, wrapping his arms around her from behind and stalling her pacing. "Easy."

Cass leaned back into his embrace, absorbing his warmth, finding solace in the strength surrounding her. She didn't need it, really. She could stand on her own two feet, take care of herself, but she appreciated it all the same.

Vicky's gone.

Taken.

A stone lodged in her throat, choking her. Vicky had always been like another little sister to her. She'd looked out for her, cared for her. To think of her missing, in danger, was intolerable. It was even worse than when they'd lost contact recently. At least then she could convince herself it was nothing, that Vicky might just be having an issue with comms. At least then she could do *something*, even if it was simply calling for help.

But there was nothing she could do now. Vicky was out there, alone, probably scared, and all she could do was just stand here, taking comfort Vicky didn't have and probably desperately needed right now.

She pushed out of Kou's arms, suddenly finding his nearness unbearable.

———

Surg paced the *Discovery's* hallway, hands fisted at his sides, as he waited for something, *anything*, from Taln's team that might help them find and retrieve Victoria.

"Would you stop that!" Taln snapped, jerking her head in his direction. Her expression was cold and lethal, a testament to her frayed nerves.

He stopped, but couldn't relax his hands. His entire body felt like a bow strung too tight, pulled back and ready to fire. "Well, what do you know? What can we do?"

"Nothing since the last time you asked two diceros ago."

He frowned. It hadn't felt like so short a time. It had felt like *ages*.

Taln sighed, standing to her feet. She walked away from where some members of her team worked diligently. "I know you're highly vested in this outcome. But we don't have a lot to work from. Almost all the systems were shut down, which means most sensors weren't even operational. The AI is working to run through any system data that was still operational at the time, but I don't hold a lot of hope there.

"I also have people working in both my ship and the *Trojan* to see if there's any data we can pull. We were all in the same area, so in theory, we might have some details on the enemy ship." She shook her head. "Whoever these guys are, though, they used some pretty advanced stealth technology. My ship was monitoring the entire space, and it should have set off an alarm if anything got anywhere near us. It didn't. That means they were using something I've never seen before."

Surg frowned. "Something you've never seen before?" It was often his business to keep an eye on what the competition was doing. And although they didn't really compete for customers, Diehli's nefarious business practices meant he had no choice but to monitor them. Ignoring them was professional suicide. It also meant he often knew what they were up to.

Or someone did. "I'm going to call headquarters. Maybe somebody there knows what they were using."

Taln nodded. "If we know what they were using, that might make all the difference."

CHAPTER TWENTY

*V*ictoria sat on the cot, thinking. She didn't know how long she'd been in the room, but so far, no one had entered. No one had offered her food or water. No one had spoken on the intercom again, either.

Fortunately, she'd found a bathroom attached to the other wall. It was tiny, with just a sink and toilet, but it was better than nothing.

Now, she just needed a plan. She rocked back and forth, her feet swaying as they dangled in front of her. She had no doubt the others would be looking for her, would try to rescue her, but she couldn't rely on that. They didn't know where she was. There was no guarantee they would find her. Even if they did, there was a possibility it wouldn't matter, that they wouldn't have the resources to retrieve her.

She couldn't wait for them.

Unfortunately, this wasn't where she excelled. She wasn't a fighter or a leader. She fell apart under stress. Hell, she even had an anxiety disorder. This was like a perfect storm for making her melt down. New environment, loss of support structure, loss of normal coping resources.

But I don't have the luxury of falling apart.

She took deep breaths, trying to slow her movements, make them more controlled, more sedate.

I have all the time in the world.

She needed to convince herself of that. She knew from experience that if she tried to push herself to move faster than she was comfortable with, she would just start spazzing out. That was when she made mistakes. That was when she stopped thinking. That was when she broke down.

"There's no time for mistakes," she muttered under her breath.

She scanned the room once more, frowning at the almost completely empty space. It was too empty. There was no equipment. This did not look like a lab intended for forced labor. In her lab back on the *Discovery*, she had a synthesizer for manufacturing parts. Here, there was nothing but a few computer terminals and cabinets.

Victoria walked over to one of the computer terminals. She woke it with a tap on the screen and sighed in relief. At least the language was Usan. Ellie had been teaching her that language on and off since she was ten. She was better at speaking it than reading it, but she could manage. Barely.

She moved through the menus. What was their plan here? What did they expect from her with no equipment? Was she supposed to requisition some?

It didn't really matter, she supposed, but if she was going to get out of here, she needed to know what her resources were. And the first step was figuring out this computer system.

Surg sat in the cockpit of the *Discovery*. He supposed he could have used the *Areon*. It was closer, but he'd still found his feet moving toward the airlock to Victoria's ship. He was drawn to her space, the last place she'd been, the last place he'd seen her.

He'd slowed as he passed through her lab space, holding his breath. A part of him had half expected to see her sitting at that workstation, back bent over her display as she worked. He stood there, waiting, listening, as if he would hear her feet tapping gently on the tiles at any moment.

But only silence answered, and he moved on. He had things to do, and even if his chest felt like a vise was clamping down on it, he had to function. He had to move on. Victoria needed him now more than ever, and he couldn't fail her. The stakes were too high.

He sat down at the console and hesitated for another moment, feeling a little surreal and out of touch with reality. "Angus, I need to make a call to headquarters."

"Aye, sir. Connecting."

He moved his focus to the screen, waiting for it to show someone's face.

"Varn," he said as his younger brother's visage filled the screen. He barely recognized him as the kid he'd been when they were first thrust out on their own. "What are you doing in my office? My assistant should have picked up."

"I'm not. I've had your calls routed to *my* office. And I think the better question is 'Why aren't *you* in *your* office?'" His brother scowled, his business attire pulling tight at his shoulders as he crossed his arms in front of him. "You've never been away from the business for this long. What is going on?"

174

He paused. Should he tell his brother everything? Should he tell him about Victoria? He wanted to, but what could he say? At this point, their relationship was nothing but a single dalliance, possibly never to be repeated. "The Diehli happened. Cass contacted me a while back about a friend of hers that had gone missing. I organized a team to help find her. It turned out the Diehli were after her. Last night, she was taken. And right out from under our noses." He closed his eyes and breathed, resisting the urge to stand and pace.

"And so you leave me to clean up your messes?"

"What messes?"

"How about the entire business? Just because you're gone, it doesn't mean things don't need to get done."

Surg hadn't thought of that at all. Sure, he'd thought about Inia Intergalactic, but he hadn't once thought about how it was doing while he was gone. He hadn't agonized over problems or who was in charge. He hadn't thought about projects or customer contracts. Since meeting Victoria, he'd been in a bubble, and those things hadn't touched him, not even when he'd reached out for assistance.

How could he have made such an about-face? How could he go from living his work to never thinking about it at all? No wonder Victoria had been so upset with him about not knowing who he was. If he'd so thoroughly pushed it from his mind, how could she have possibly guessed?

"I'm sorry, Varn. This is important."

"More important than your business?" Varn said, sounding skeptical.

Surg thought of all the loneliness, all the isolation. "Yes." When he'd met Cass, things had started to change. She didn't defer to him or treat him as superior. She knew he was a big time businessman, but that didn't matter to her. He'd found it refreshing. He'd seen someone he could be friends with, her and Kou.

But what made me open up to them? What made me reach out and try for the first time in far too long? Why did I play matchmaker?

He saw people at all stages of their lives, of their relationships, but he'd never felt inclined before to step in, to intervene. Why had he done it then? What had been different? Was it the lack of formality? Or was it something else?

And why had he gone after that lead himself? He could have sent his team. He could have delegated, but he hadn't. And if he had, he might never have met Victoria. That would have been a shame.

"Varn, I know you don't understand. This is important to me. And something definitely needs to be done about the Diehli."

"Well, that's the first sensible thing you've said. Do you have a plan?"

He shook his head. "No. The people that took Victoria. We can't figure out how they did it. First, they used stealth technology Taln's team has never seen before. They can't even pinpoint the ship's former location from sensor data after the fact. Then, they somehow managed to shut off all the systems necessary to keep themselves undetectable by the *Discovery*."

"The *Discovery*?"

"Yes, that's Victoria's ship. It's an Earth word."

"Right." Varn looked away from the camera, tapping his thumb over his hand idly as he thought. "I'll get back to you. I have to talk to some of our scientists in person. But I definitely think I've heard of this stealth technology before. I've been putting out feelers on how to acquire it, but none of my contacts have had any luck so far. I think it might be technology the Diehli pioneered, which would be a problem."

Surg nodded. "Because maybe no one else has it."

"Which means you might be out of luck on tracking that ship."

CHAPTER TWENTY-ONE

*V*ictoria stared at the device that dominated the once empty countertop. It was large and bulky, like a big 3D printer, which was essentially what it was. The plan had seemed so simple once the idea came to her.

They don't know English.

And she didn't have to give them what they wanted just because they asked for it. In fact, they didn't know much of anything about the device they'd asked her to make. She could probably make pretty much anything, and they wouldn't be able to tell. The thought warmed her up inside. She tried to keep her expression neutral, but a smile itched at the edges of her lips. No one had ever made a device like she'd designed. If she made the components sufficiently strange looking, they shouldn't know the difference.

It helped that they didn't know English, and what little programming she could do was *all* in English. Humans didn't speak Earth languages around aliens, for the most part. They hadn't since their first alliance with the Incirrina. And the Incirrina had taught them Uso. Since then, only the Danaus had needed to communicate in English, and that was because their species didn't have interstellar travel of their own. They had to either learn a human language, or a human would have to learn their own. Uso wasn't a practical option.

So there was no reason any of them should understand her coding. She knew a lot about her ships, everything, in fact. She didn't need schematics and diagrams to build things. Many of them, she could just pull up in her head, like a great big library just waiting for her to check out a book.

I can do this.

It would be simple, nerve-wracking, but simple. She just needed to go at her own pace, take her time. She could do anything if she just took her time.

Step 1: Plan out her code in English.

Step 2: Design parts on the computer, disguising her purpose.

And Step 3: Build it and call for help.

After all, if anyone could build an emergency beacon targeted to only *her* ships, it would be her.

Easy as pie.

"Incoming call from Inia Intergalactic," Angus said, breaking Surg out of his thoughts.

"What?"

"Would you like to answer?"

"Yes, of course." He sat up straighter in his seat in the *Discovery's* cockpit, tugging at his hopelessly rumpled clothing. Time seemed to have become nonsensical since the moment he'd realized Victoria was missing. He couldn't even remember the last time he'd showered. How long had it been? It could have been hours but he suspected it was days. It felt like a lifetime.

"Brother," Varn said, exposing his neck in the standard greeting.

Surg reciprocated, already feeling better about this conversation. His brother was in a better mood if he was being respectful from the start. "Have you found anything?"

"Maybe. Quite a few ships have been hit by a ship with the technology you mentioned." He shook his head. "And there hasn't been any whisperings on the black market about selling anything like it, which tells me it's most likely developed by the Diehli. And they're keeping it to themselves. It's a smart move. Definitely gives them an advantage business-wise. And with the type of clientele they deal with, it gives them a little bit of leverage. 'You'll never see us coming,' " Varn said, rolling his eyes.

"None of that sounds like good news, or explains the maybe."

"I was getting to that. It may be nothing, but the scientists *have* an idea about how to detect these ships. They just haven't had an opportunity to test it."

"Perfect. Send it our way."

"Not so fast, brother. This isn't like sending Taln's team out to assist. These are scientists. We have to ensure their safety."

"Of course. Do you honestly think I wouldn't look after my own people?"

"I don't know what's going through your head right now, but it's certainly not putting the company or any of us first."

"How can you say that?" Surg said in outrage.

Varn shook his head, scowling. "I don't know. Maybe because you jumped at the first solution without us even coming up with a proper plan. You're not focusing on the details like you usually do. That's not who my brother is."

Surg sagged. "You're right. My head isn't in the game. I'm sorry."

"It's okay. Just tell me what's going on. Is this a new acquisition? You know, you usually include me on those things." He smirked.

"No." Surg tried to think like a businessman, but it was surprisingly hard. He struggled to think of anything but Victoria. Was she okay? Where was she? He pulled his thoughts together. He needed to focus. "But we can't afford the Diehli to get their hands on this technology either."

"What type of technology?"

"Instantaneous travel." There was a long pause, and Surg wondered for a moment if the connection had glitched. "Varn?"

Varn shook himself. "Sorry, that's… are you serious?"

Surg nodded, his throat tight.

"That's groundbreaking. If we could get our hands on that…"

"Don't even think about it," Surg snapped, suddenly furious with his brother. "It's not ours to take."

"Easy." Varn raised his hands, leaning slightly away from the camera. "Of course, it's not. We're not the Diehli." He reached up and rubbed his ear as he thought. It was a little gesture he'd been doing since he was a little kid, and it made Surg smile. He shook his head as his hand dropped. "We can't let this get into their hands. There's no telling what they would do with this type of technology."

"I know."

"And the inventor is this Victoria you mentioned?"

"Yes." He hated boiling her existence down to that one element. It felt cold. It made him feel dangerously close to the person she was afraid he might be, the same person he was determined to prove he wasn't.

His brother nodded on screen. "And they must have used the stealth ship to get her. So if we do this right, we can rescue her, keep her invention out of Diehli hands, *and* get our hands on that proprietary stealth tech." Varn grinned, the expression looking just a little ruthless.

"Good. That's good." He didn't much care about anything but Victoria, but if it got his brother on board, he was game.

CHAPTER TWENTY-TWO

*T*ime passed slowly in captivity, even when she had work to do. Victoria was tracking her time here by her energy levels and how many meals they'd sent her. She had only the most rudimentary understanding of their time system and had no idea how to translate it to Earth time, so it was the best she could do. By her estimate, it had been a couple days.

The food was slop, barely edible, and she picked at it more than ate it. Usually, she waited until she couldn't think straight anymore before taking a break, which was just plain stupid. Victoria knew from experience what happened when she worked too much. She started getting tense and frustrated, sometimes from hunger, sometimes from fatigue, but other times from lack of exercise.

She'd just finished a break, and now she stared at her computer screen, feeling a little more centered, more focused. Still, she couldn't help feeling like someone was staring at her, watching her. Her skin crawled, and she just wanted to curl up in a ball and hide. But that wasn't an option.

I won't get away with this.

That was a constant refrain in her mind. How could she possibly fool these people? What was she thinking? She was going to get herself killed.

Except she knew they wouldn't kill her. If she screwed up, it wouldn't be Victoria who would paid the price. They'd known where to find her. They would find her friends.

So, don't screw up.

She focused again on the task at hand. It shouldn't have been hard. She'd always retreated into her studies, her research, when stressed. This would be no different. She went over the designs, reviewing them in exploded view, checking all the parts. Was there anything off? She needed to disguise the beacon as something that resembled an engine. With her knowledge, it shouldn't be that hard. Engines often came with sensor arrays that sent information to the central computer or AI for repairs and maintenance during flight. All she was doing was adding an extra part. She already planned to have it hooked up to the computer to control and monitor its function. That was to be expected for testing an engine prototype.

They wouldn't notice. How could they? She was just going to install a stronger transmitter than she would normally employ. And it had to be a wireless transmitter instead of wired, but those were the only differences. Just little things. Barely anything, really.

They wouldn't notice, would they?

She hoped not.

Surg stood at the airlock. The second team had just arrived, attaching to the *Discovery* only moments ago. The plan was for the scientific team to explore this ship first, then move on to the other ships if necessary.

A moment later, the door hissed open. "Varn. I didn't realize you were going to come, too."

His little brother smiled, stepping through and wrapping him in a one-armed hug. "Don't worry. The company is in good hands while we're gone, and I don't intend to be away for long. I did, however, feel like we should work together on this. What you're dealing with here is huge, and I think we need to put our full focus on it."

He nodded, appreciating his brother's support and taking comfort in the weight of his arm. "Let's get started."

The scientists spilled out into the lab space, their eyes lighting up, though he couldn't say what they seemed so excited about. It was just a room, one like many others he'd encountered in his life. After the scientists, a security team entered, tense and alert.

"I see you brought reinforcements."

Varn dropped his arm. "One can never be too careful, especially when dealing with the Diehli. They're slimy bastards, more than happy to use any means necessary to get what they want. I don't plan to let them."

But would it be enough? Two teams and four ships against the Diehli? What if Victoria was already at their headquarters? It had been days. She could be anywhere by now.

I should have gone after her. What am I waiting for?

But where would he have looked? Where would he have gone? He had this idiotic urge to just search everywhere, but that wouldn't help her. That wouldn't help anyone. He needed to be smart, careful, practical.

"So what *do* you plan to do?" he said, glancing over his shoulder at his brother.

"Whatever it takes. We need to track down this stealth technology."

"And if that doesn't work? What if they can't detect it?"

Varn looked over at him. "We'll come to that if we need to."

Meaning he didn't have a clue.

CHAPTER TWENTY-THREE

*B*ehind Victoria, the 3D printer was hard at work. It had been churning out parts for hours. It whirred and clicked and beeped. With each part completed, she moved on to the next, initiating another round of printing.

After removing each part from the printer, she rotated it in her hands, checking for flaws and edges to smooth. The weight always surprised her. She picked up her file and sat down on the cot, working out a bur on the latest part. It was the second to last. She just had one more part left printing. She'd been assembling as she went, so there was a large device on a scaffold in the middle of the room. It was big, metal, and looked a lot like an engine.

The 3D printer beeped once more, signaling it had finished the final part. Victoria stood, walking to the "engine" with the part she'd been filing down in hand. Finding where it belonged, she socketed it in place smoothly before returning to the printer and pulling open the small, acrylic door to remove the last part.

She rotated it in her hand, looking for imperfections, but found none. It was heavy, a bit sharp on some of the edges, but not outside of specs.

Did I make a mistake?

She stood in front of the printer, not moving as she second-guessed herself. She'd thought of initiating the signal earlier, but was afraid they would question it if she tested the software without building sufficient parts to go with it. But had she gone too far? Would they take what they could get and try to figure out the software on their own?

Except, software was half the battle. Without the right calculations, the hardware, even if it actually *was* the hardware they wanted, would be useless. And her work so far had been highly theoretical. There was no way she could solve it in one try. If they knew anything about science, they would know that.

She just hoped they knew something about science.

Victoria moved over to the scaffolding. Reaching in, she put the final piece in place. It clicked as it settled in. She let out a deep breath before moving back to the computer terminal. The screen was still mostly in Usan, though the programming window read a bunch of human programming language. While waiting for each part to print, she'd alternated between filing down burs and working on the code she needed to make this work, tweaking it again and again. Now, she just had to run the script.

Her fingers hovered over the screen. This was it, the moment. The point of no return. Once she did this, she couldn't take it back.

Am I killing my friends?

She would rather die than do that.

Shock hit her, and she stepped back, surprised.

I would rather die?

It didn't make any sense. She'd always preferred being alone. Even when she'd lived with others, she'd always tried to find little spots of isolation. She'd never really understood the attachment people felt for other people, the importance they gave it in their lives. Perhaps that was why she'd had no problem launching herself into space, living a life of complete solitude.

So why would she rather die than risk her friends? Did they really mean that much to her? She tried to work her mind through it logically, her fingers idly tapping her thighs, but she couldn't figure it out. Logic failed her. For the first time in her life, logic failed her. She didn't want to die, but she couldn't fathom them dying either.

Especially Surg.

When she thought of each of them, imagining them dead, Surg's death stopped her cold. She couldn't get beyond it. Her chest tightened up, and she wanted to collapse to the floor, but she couldn't let herself. The stakes were too high.

She stood pressed against the central table, staring at the computer screen, the script's icon staring back at her defiantly.

Just do it, Vic. Just do it.

She closed her eyes, took a deep breath, and opened them, reaching forward to execute the command.

———

"I think we found something!" one of the scientists yelled, her voice almost squeaky with her excitement.

Surg jerked his head up, having mostly nodded off. The systems on the *Discovery* were useless, the sensors and databases offline during much of the time they'd needed to analyze. Also, the scientists hadn't been familiar with the programming language, which had left them at a disadvantage.

So, they'd quickly moved to the *Areon*. Taln had been pacing in his peripheral vision for hours. He, Taln, and Varn had been in the ship's meeting room waiting. He and Varn were used to having to wait from time to time. Varn had been going over communications and contracts while Surg had sat back with his legs propped up on the central table. Taln, however, was *not* used to waiting.

Surg yawned and sat up. "What have you got?"

The scientist practically vibrated with excitement. "Well, it's impossible for anything to give off *no* signal, right?"

"Sure?" Surg shrugged.

"Anyway, it's impossible to give off no signal. It's impossible to go completely undetected. The problem is we don't know how to detect it. We don't know what to look for. But even that is telling. If we know what our systems *are* looking for, and we know we're not detecting anything, but we know something is there, then we also know where the gaps are."

"Gaps. You're coming to us with gaps?" Taln said, stopping in place, her expression stern, almost menacing.

"Yes, I am," the scientist said with a smile, pointing a finger at Taln.

Taln scowled.

"Anyway, there's a lot more information received from our sensors than our systems analyze. Most of it gets automatically ignored because it's just background noise. But…" She held up a finger. "… if we look for gaps in the background noise, we can find something." She turned her back on them, touching the wall to wake up the built-in screen.

The display came alive, and she moved through menus and windows until she pulled up two images. They just looked like an image of the *Discovery*.

"Not sure what I'm seeing," Surg said.

"This is an image taken from our sensors before the kidnapping. Now, we know at some point, a ship docked with the *Discovery*. We had a starting point, since that was when the systems first malfunctioned, and they stopped recording to their databases.

"From there, we were able to create a timeframe when we most expected that ship might have been docked." The scientist grinned. "It's really cool. Now, I'm going to bring up a second image."

They all nodded.

She touched the screen, opening a new image on the right. This one showed again an image of the *Discovery*, but this time, they couldn't see a large segment of it.

"What am I looking at?" Surg leaned forward, his elbows pressing into the table in front of him.

"This is an overlay of two different sensors. During this time period, the visual sensors still saw what they were supposed to see, but some of the other sensors were coming up completely blank. So there was a signal telling your ship that this image existed, but there were other indicators that were getting completely wiped clean. In fact," she pointed at the picture on the left, "they actually screwed up. This stealth technology is good, really good, but it has one inherent flaw. It hides its own signal, and in so doing, hides the signal of other things around it. They knew to replicate images behind them so they would go undetected, but they screwed up on the rest of the stuff."

"Then, can we track it?" Surg shifted in his seat, trying to keep calm and steady, but he just wanted to jump into action, to start the chase *now*.

The scientist nodded. "With sufficient data, yes. We were able to determine their direction to the limit of your sensors, but if we want to follow them, we really need more information. We need to access sensors that were running when the ship was passing. It'll take a lot of math to find them, but doable."

"Then they don't leave a trail?"

She rubbed her forehead. "I don't know. Maybe. But, I mean, we're days out. Any residual trail would be gone by now. My suggestion is creating a projected path based on the initial direction of travel, which we have. Maybe we can create a hypothesis on where they might be going and reach out to ships along that path asking for sensor data to analyze. If we know the direction they're going and their approximate speed, we can estimate where they'll be, confirm using sensor data from other ships and stations, and determine their destination."

"Do it."

CHAPTER TWENTY-FOUR

$\mathcal{V}$ ictoria continued to pretend to test her "instantaneous travel engine." She ran simulations on the computer and jotted down notes, tweaked fake code, and ran additional simulations. When the engine "failed" to transport something, she cursed, throwing a little fit for the cameras.

She needed them to believe she was trying.

The door opened behind her, and she jumped. In the entire time she'd been there, the door hadn't opened once when she was conscious. She suspected they'd drugged her to put the 3D printer in the room. They delivered food remotely through a slot. Everything else was provided for her in the room. They never had to enter, so why now?

Victoria spun around and swallowed hard. She kept her hands planted firmly at her sides, making a conscious effort to keep them still. She breathed slowly, trying to relax her body and keep herself calm. It didn't work, but she tried anyway.

"Can I help you?"

"Tell me about your progress." The person stepped further into the room. Their expression was mild, neutral, but there was something about them that was alarming. She wanted to run, but nothing about the person overtly screamed danger.

"Slow. When you *kidnapped* me, I wasn't far enough along in my research." She waved her hand at the "device" she'd made. "I tried building it, but I'm still not having any luck. I'd barely gotten beyond the initial design phases. Calculations and theoretical designs, really. I'd only *barely* gotten started with the programming, and I usually get help with that."

"You're lying." The person's expression didn't change.

"No, I'm not." She really wasn't. She was nowhere close to building a full prototype when she was taken. It would have taken months, maybe even years, to get a working system from that. She wasn't working from the backbones of already functioning systems here like she had in the past. She was creating something entirely new, never seen before. "I have no idea how long this will take. The science behind it is sound. I'm positive it will work with enough experimentation, but it's gonna take time."

"If you were trying."

Victoria shook her head. She didn't know what to do. She didn't know what to say. Her breath caught in her throat, choking off words. "I *am* trying," she finally got out. Her face burned, tears welling up in her eyes. She was frustrated and scared, and she hoped her emotions could be somehow misconstrued.

The intruder slowly shook its head, tsking. "You're not. You're waiting for your friends to rescue you. You're biding your time."

"Wha-why would you even think that?"

They leaned into her personal space, and Victoria backed up, bumping into the counter behind her. "Because we detected your signal."

Victoria froze, her entire body thrumming with fear. For a moment, she couldn't think, couldn't process anything. Her hands were the first to move, though not in any controlled way. They just trembled, and she gripped onto the counter, her fingers bumping into a part she'd been playing with. She'd removed in from the "engine" to "fix" it. "What signal?" she whispered, her fingers shaking as she inched closer to the part.

"Don't play coy with me. We expected you to try something like this, but you can't fool us. We *always* get what we want."

Her fingers wrapped around the cold metal, and she swung out, closing her eyes as her arm made a wide arc. Someone grunted, and she could breathe again. She dropped the metal. It clattered to the floor. Her breathing was ragged, and she took several more breaths with her eyes closed before finally opening them and looking down.

For a moment, she couldn't believe her eyes. She wasn't a violent person. Never had been. Sure, she'd been told she had a temper, and she'd had her share of tantrums growing up, but she'd never been quick to anger, and even slower to aggression. She'd never hit someone before.

But there they were, her victim, laying on the ground like a limp doll, a black smudge staining the floor. A little blood trickled from their forehead.

"What have I done?" She held her head in both hands, wanting to pace, wanting to move, but that wouldn't solve her problems. She needed to do something. What would they do when they found out she'd attacked one of their own? She glanced up at the camera in the corner. They probably already knew.

I don't have a lot of time.

Victoria felt like a train with its motor running, but it wasn't on a set of tracks. She couldn't figure out where to go, what to do. She needed to get out of here, but the door was locked. She couldn't get out.

Or could she?

She squatted down next to the person she'd assaulted. "Sorry," she said under her breath. She patted them down. Maybe they had a key, an ID, something that would open the door. She hoped to hell there wasn't someone on the other side of that camera deciding when to open and close the door. If so, she was screwed.

There was something hard in a back pocket. She reached in, the material scraping against the back of her hand, and pulled it out. It looked like a square piece of plastic, but it had a logo on it. She looked up at the door, but didn't see a sensor beside it. She turned the square in her hand, checking it on all sides. Back on Earth, they'd used ID badges for controlled access, but they'd required a sensor next to the door, right? At least, they had at all the places she'd worked.

Victoria stood up, walking hesitantly toward the door. Maybe this one worked differently. Maybe the sensor wasn't visible. After all, a sensor you could see was a sensor you could access, hack, short-circuit. She approached the door with her heart pounding.

It's not going to open.

Her unoccupied hand ran over the central island, the slick surface centering her a bit.

It has to work.

Before she reached the door, it opened, and she stopped, surprised, but also scared. What if there was someone in the hallway? What if they saw her, attacked her, chased her?

Then you run.

She peeked her head out, but the hallway was blissfully empty. "Thank God."

Each direction looked the same. Which way should she go? She didn't know this ship and wasn't awake when they brought her here. Hell, she didn't even know if it *was* a ship, though the design was certainly similar.

It didn't matter, she told herself. She needed to find a place to hide and wait until her friends arrived. She took a left, running her hand along the wall and waving the card, hoping for a door to open and present the perfect hiding place. Some doors, she avoided. She could read Usan, and they were labeled. Personal quarters were likely to be locked for individuals. Conversely, things like medical, meeting rooms, and such could probably be opened with her key, but were also likely to have people in them or have people show up without notice, leaving her trapped. She needed somewhere she could hide, but also somewhere people were less likely to go.

Like a maintenance corridor.

Surg sat in the cockpit of the *Discovery* feeling bored. He had nothing to do. They were following the calculated trajectory of the stealth ship while they reached out to anything along the path that might have sensor data they could use. The scientists were busy trying to track the ship using that data.

But that left Surg with nothing to do but think, staring out into space. His feet were propped up on the console, but he wasn't at ease. He was worried about Victoria. They were so far behind. So much could have happened since then. Was she even alive?

"Surg?" Angus said.

"Yes?" He dropped his feet, the soles of his boots slapping against the floor with a resounding clap.

"I'm getting a signal. It's a distress beacon, and it seems to be targeted specifically at this class of ship."

"What?" He leaned forward. How was that possible? "What does it say?"

"It doesn't appear to say anything. I've tracked it back to these coordinates." Angus brought up a map image of a location in space.

"That's Diehli headquarters."

A moment passed, then Angus spoke up again. "Aye, my database access seems to concur with that conclusion."

"Who would be sending us a distress beacon from Diehli headquarters?" But the answer occurred to him before even Angus could respond. "Victoria." She somehow found a way to call for help. "Get the others on the line. Now. We know where to go."

"Aye, sir."

The screen erupted into three windows that almost immediately connected.

"I received a distress signal from Vicky," Cass said the moment the connection completed.

"I did, too," Surg said, feeling hopeful for the first time in days.

"So you think you know where your inventor is?" Varn sounded skeptical. "What if this distress signal is just intended to throw us off their trail? Isn't this a little convenient?"

Cass scoffed. "You don't know Vicky."

"You're right. I don't. But I do know the Diehli. I know what they're capable of. And sending a distress signal to the wrong location, to a trap, is just the type of thing they would do. We should follow the stealth ship's trajectory. We *know* that will bring us where we need to go. That's the only place we know she's been. Better to play it safe."

Surg didn't want to play it safe, though. He wanted to rescue Victoria. "And what if by playing it safe the Diehli gets what they want? Or Victoria dies. What then?" And then a new thought occurred to him. What if all his brother cared about was that stealth technology? What if he would gladly sacrifice Victoria to get it?

He hated thinking that, even for a moment. It sounded so cutthroat. He had a hard time believing it of his brother. He'd raised him better, hadn't he? But then, did he really even *know* Varn anymore? They'd grown so distant over the years. Surg had spent so much of his life building that stupid company, but what had he really accomplished? Sure, they had financial security, but that wasn't everything, was it? He hadn't been happy. Was his brother? Or had he locked his only remaining family into a life he might not even want?

They never talked about anything personal anymore, so he didn't even know. How could he? And how could he fix it? Certainly not now, when they were on other ships, with a half-dozen people listening in.

"I think you need to calm down, Surg," Varn said, expressing the same level of calm Surg usually felt.

Because I had nothing to lose.

"Fuck that," Cass snapped, drawing everyone's attention. "This signal *definitely* came from Vicky. It was sent directly to our ships and *only* our ships. I'm not even sure *I* could do that, and I programmed the damned things. The *only* way to do that would be with an extensive understanding of our hardware. People at Diehli could threaten her into sending a signal to draw us there, but that doesn't mean she would have to make it so targeted. In fact, she could probably send it so that it specifically missed us, and they wouldn't have any way to know that. She *sent* this."

"I agree," Surg said, sitting up taller and turning to the screen showing his brother.

Varn scowled, his shoulders growing visibly tenser.

"Down, boys," Taln said from her ship, looking like she wanted to roll her eyes. "There's an easy way to solve this. Surg, where is the distress signal coming from?"

"Diehli headquarters."

"Perfect," she glared at the camera. "That's the trajectory of the stealth ship. Varn? Your team and ship will continue to monitor data on the stealth ship's path as it comes in. Let us all know if it changes. We can make a decision *if* the time comes that we need to. Until then, there's no decision to make. There's no point arguing about this."

"Thank you, Taln," Surg said, finally feeling like they were on the right path, like he would soon have Victoria safe once more.

Only, if she was at Diehli headquarters, they were going to have to figure out a way to get her out. And that would be no easy task.

In fact, it would be an impossible one.

CHAPTER TWENTY-FIVE

 *hey'll find me.*

They'll rescue me.

Victoria had to keep reminding herself of that. She knew they would come for her. She'd sent the signal. There was no way Angus wouldn't detect it. It was designed to target his programming specifically.

They know where I am.

Of course, that wasn't the main problem now. No, the problem now was that she was hiding in a maintenance closet aboard a ship or station, most likely owned by the Diehli. They had to know she was missing, which also meant they had to be looking for her. How long until they found her?

The closet was small and cramped. The floor was hard and cold, digging into her butt painfully and making her want to get up, but the space was so small she wouldn't get two steps before hitting a wall. That fact, and the situation at hand, made her feel claustrophobic, like everything was closing in on her, ready to strangle her. It probably didn't help that the walls were a maze of jumbled, bundled wires behind mesh panels. It matched her mind.

Her thoughts felt chaotic, and she closed her eyes, trying to just *be* for a while.

There's time.

Calm down.

There's no need to fly off the handle.

She opened her eyes and felt calmer, but her thoughts still thrashed inside her head like a sack of hissing cats. She wanted to escape, to retreat somewhere safe, but there was nowhere to go.

Her parents would have retreated into their faiths, but she'd never really believed. Her mother's Christianity was too filled with contradictions, and the fanaticism of some of their members disturbed her. She'd always connected more with her father's Taoism, but could never quite get the hang of it or understand the full breadth of it. Both religions had their merits, moral lessons and suggestions on ways of living that could be practically applied, but there was always a point where things broke down for her, leaving her frustrated.

In the end, it didn't matter, though. Religion had never helped her, not even as an escape. The only escape she'd ever known was her obsession, and she couldn't indulge in it now. There was no lab to go to, just this tiny closet.

She rocked in place, her arms wrapped around her knees. It relieved some of the pain in her tailbone and helped with the urge to move.

They'll find me.

They'll rescue me.

"You have an incoming call," Angus said.

Surg was standing in Victoria's room. He'd been in it so few times, it seemed foreign and even more so because Victoria wasn't here. With nothing better to do, he'd wandered in here, wanting to feel connected to her, if only for a few moments.

He cleared his throat. "Put it through."

The wall next to him changed, making a call window in the middle. "Varn."

His brother looked serious, like he had a difficult topic to broach. "Surg, we need to talk."

"About what?" He leaned against one of the comfy chairs near the wall. The chair looked like it could engulf someone as short as Victoria.

Huh. He never thought about just how small she was, but she was drastically shorter than him. She just seemed so much larger in his perceptions.

"Where is your head at lately? We have two huge potential acquisitions, but you don't seem to care. What's going on?"

"Acquisitions? A woman's life is in danger, and you're worried about acquisitions?" Surg stepped back from the chair, his hands fisting at his sides. "Where's *your* head at?"

"Surg…"

"No, Varn. Just no. We are better than the Diehli, and part of the reason we are is that we hold ourselves to higher standards. I *could* have set up shop like the Diehli and put our headquarters outside of the reign of any government. I didn't. I *could* have allowed my employees to use questionable tactics to get what we want. I don't. How we do things matter, Varn."

"I know that. You think I don't?" He looked away from the camera, mouth agape, as he shook his head. "I've always respected the way you do business, Surg. In spite of not being willing to resort to underhanded tactics, you've still managed to make a roaring success of Inia Intergalactic."

"And yet you're so focused on the acquisitions, you're forgetting about the people involved. I already told you. Victoria's technology is *not* an acquisition."

"But it could be. It could be, and you're too blind to see it. You're never like that. You always see the opportunities."

"You still don't get it. I see the opportunities when people are willing. She's *not*. I know she's not. And it doesn't matter. I don't care about a new acquisition. I just want her safe. I'm sorry, but I'm going to save her. No matter what it takes."

CHAPTER TWENTY-SIX

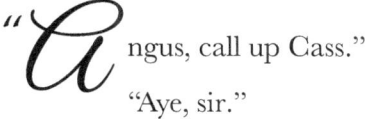"ngus, call up Cass."

"Aye, sir."

Surg had just hung up on his brother. He couldn't believe he'd done it. He couldn't believe the words that had come out of his mouth. Inia Intergalactic had been his life for so long that he didn't know any other way to live, and he'd practically turned his back on it.

"Surg," Cass said as her face showed up on the wall. "What are you doing in Victoria's room?"

He looked around him, only then remembering where he was. "I guess I missed her."

She smirked. "You like her. A lot."

"Yes." He lifted his chin. She meant the world to him.

"Do you love her?" She leaned forward, like someone eager for some gossip.

He paused, his chest squeezing with emotion. "Yes," he said under his breath, speaking it almost reverently.

Her grin grew. "I *knew* it."

Surg frowned. "Is this really the most important thing to be discussing right now?"

"Well, no, but until we get there, what else is there to do?"

"Figure out how to get there faster?"

She leaned back in her chair, running her hand through her short, purple hair. "Not really my forte." She looked away, shaking her head.

"What?"

"I was just thinking that Vicky would be the one to know." She laughed, but there was no humor in it. "Angus, is there any way that we can get there faster?"

"Aye, but the other ships cannot."

"What do you mean?" Surg stepped closer to the screen. "What can we do that they can't?"

"Sub-space. These ships are designed to travel most of the time in sub-space. Because we were receiving constant data from other ships on what trajectory to travel, we couldn't use those engines. But if we don't need that data, we can get there significantly quicker."

"How much quicker?" He didn't know anything about sub-space. It was an Earth tech. People tended to largely ignore it because humans were so new to interstellar travel.

"A few hours," Angus chimed in.

"Hours?" He wracked his brain, trying to remember the conversion between hours and horos. Less than an horo, he knew that. How could that be? "But it would take ernos at our current speed."

"Ernos. That's like a day, right?" Cass asked.

"Yes," Angus replied. "One ernos is 25 Earth hours."

Surg had mostly tuned out the conversation. Sub-space was that fast? He didn't see how it could be possible. He'd always thought of the sub-space engines as little more than children's toys while everyone else was playing with the real thing, but if they could accomplish that, he'd terribly underestimated them.

"Well, damn," Cass said. "That means if we do this, we can't rely on the others. We have to do it alone."

"Maybe not," Surg said. "Angus, can you connect with Taln?"

"Aye, sir."

A second window popped up on the wall, waiting to connect.

"What do you think Taln can do? Her ship can't keep up."

"True, but maybe it doesn't have to."

"What are you thinking?"

The second window changed. "Surg, sir. How can I help you?"

He leaned forward and gripped the back of the chair, his fingers digging into the plush material. "We have a way that we can get to Diehli headquarters significantly faster."

"You're reconsidering the decision to keep together until the trail deviates?"

"Yes. I think it's a safe bet. With two of our ships able to get there in a matter of hours rather than days, it reduces the risk in case Victoria is at Diehli headquarters."

"The human ships?"

"Yes. Sub-space engines."

She rolled her eyes. "Of course." Then she shook her head. "It won't work, though. Those ships do *not* have any stealth technologies. They'll be spotted the moment they drop out of sub-space. You'll never get close."

"Damn," Cass said, spinning away from the camera.

"However," Taln said, looking thoughtful. "We might be able to transfer some of the tech from my ship."

"You can do that?" Cass said, turning back.

"Well, it would certainly be easier than moving an engine."

Jessie snorted, making Surg realize she was in on the call. "How long would it take?"

"I'll have to check. Get back to you within an horo?"

"We'll be waiting." He leaned back. An horo was going to feel like an eternity.

Eventually, Victoria calmed down. Her ass still hurt from sitting on the hard floor, but at least the walls weren't closing in on her. Problem was, now that she wasn't freaking out, logic surged back with a vengeance. It was her saving grace and her curse. Logic didn't sugarcoat things. It followed the path of evidence and reasoning, eventually reaching a final conclusion. It meant she could take comfort in the fact that her friends would search for her, but it also told her that the chances of them succeeding in rescuing her were practically nonexistent.

When she'd run through the halls looking for a place to hide, she hadn't seen much, but she already knew a few things. First, whatever this place was, it was huge. That meant even a small team would probably have trouble infiltrating it without getting noticed. Second, she suspected this place was owned by the Diehli. From what she'd gathered, it was a big and ruthless company. That meant they wouldn't skimp on security because people that immoral tended to believe everyone else was, too.

So, most likely she was in either a large ship, probably holding hundreds of people or a space station that could hold thousands easily. Neither was a good option. They had Taln's security forces, and Cass was adept at getting into places undetected, being that she was a pirate, but would that be enough?

She stood up, reexamining the room. Maybe she could do something, make it easier for them somehow.

"Well, if I'm going to help them, I need to know what I have available to me." Other than the bundles of wires, though, the only thing in the room was a single display panel. It took a single step to put herself in front of it. She touched it and smiled. The screen lit up, showing a bunch of maintenance menus. Her smile grew.

Oh, this'll do nicely.

"Okay, I'm back," Taln said.

Surg had been waiting impatiently since their last call had ended.

Taln settled into her seat, having initiated the call even before she was ready, it would seem. "We need to transfer the software to the *Trojan*, but then it's just a matter of transferring personnel and tech. We should be able to install the stealth hardware while we're on the way there.

"Perfect," Cass said, a grin on her face. "Welcome aboard!"

"I'll contact Varn's ship, then have Angus pilot the *Discovery*. Once I'm done, I'll meet you guys on the *Trojan*," Surg said.

"Looks like we have a plan." Taln nodded and disconnected.

"See you in a few, Surg."

Surg nodded and ended the comm. He sighed and leaned forward, not looking forward to the next call. It seemed inevitable that it wouldn't go well. How could it? None of the conversations he'd had recently with his brother *had*. "No point putting it off. Angus call Varn's ship."

"Aye, sir."

The screen changed, and it took a few moments for the call to go through. "Surg."

"Varn. Change of plans."

"What do you mean 'change of plans'?"

"We're going to use the sub-space engine on the *Trojan* to get to Diehli headquarters faster."

"We talked about this. We said we'd continue along this path and reevaluate if it deviated."

"And it'll take days to get there. What if she doesn't have days? It already took so long to get to this point. There's no telling what could have happened already." He took in a deep breath, determined not to get in an argument. "We're going to take some of the tech from the *Areon* to boost the stealth capabilities of the *Trojan*. The *Trojan* will continue ahead in sub-space while the rest of the ships continue on with you in the lead."

"Stop. Just stop." Varn shook his head. "I don't get you anymore. We had a plan. It was solid, careful, and you just want to go barreling forward? This is not smart. This is not how we do business. We're careful and methodical. We look at all the angles."

"This isn't business, Varn. This is life. Life is not neat. It can't be carefully compartmentalized and organized so everything has its place and all the risks can be analyzed and minimized. Sometimes there's no other choice."

"Yes, there is. We can follow the same plan we already had. She'll be fine. What are they going to do to her in a couple days?"

"You *know* the Diehli. They could do anything to her in a couple days."

CHAPTER TWENTY-SEVEN

ictoria paced her small room.

One... two... turn... one... two... turn...

It was agonizing, fraying her nerves.

What if I screwed up?

What if they trace what I did back to this terminal?

What if they find me?

The room was too small. Each time she made a circuit, it felt like her nerves were wound even tighter than before. Plus, there was nowhere to go. If they found her, she would be trapped. There was no back way out of this room. This was it.

Maybe I should move.

Except, moving was dangerous, too. What if she was spotted in the hallways? What if she couldn't find another place to hide? She would be a sitting duck.

Then again, wasn't she already a sitting duck?

Victoria turned back to the terminal on the wall. There had to be something in there that would help her. Maybe she could find a way to access security or surveillance. Maybe she could get a full blueprint or map of this place. Either would help her. Both would be preferable.

She woke up the screen, going through the menus one by one. Electrical. Water. Air. Propulsion. If there was propulsion, it was probably a ship. Or maybe not. Her Usan wasn't the best. Maybe it was referring to thrusters. Didn't space stations have thrusters for minute corrections or artificial gravity?

She sighed, still feeling like she knew nothing about her situation.

I really need to improve my Usan. This is ridiculous.

She continued through the menus. "Bingo." She pulled up a map, which had been hiding in a help menu.

Go figure.

"Now, how do I get out of here?"

Cass stood behind a team of techs while they installed the stealth devices in the guts of her ship. She didn't like it. People were adding things to the *Trojan* she didn't understand. Sure, she rarely understood Victoria's technobabble, but she trusted her. She didn't know these people.

Behind her, she could hear Taln and Kou coordinating the team, trying to come up with a plan of attack. A stab of jealousy hit her. They worked so well together, seemed so in sync.

And we're not.

She and Kou usually fought, their life views so diametrically opposed that they rarely ever saw eye to eye on anything.

It works for us.

She tried to reassure herself, but this time it wasn't working. Taln's voice rang through the corridor, with Kou's deeper one humming along in harmony with it like a beautiful song.

She turned back to the techs, her jaw tense. "What's our status?"

"One moment." The two were nothing more than moving shadows, highlighted by their work lights. "There. All set. Should work."

"Great." She turned and stomped off. "Angus, I want you to test the new systems. Make sure everything's operational."

"Aye, lass."

As soon as Cass stepped into the light, Kou looked up and smiled. Her worries dropped away for a little while, and she walked over next to him.

He wrapped an arm around her, pulling her close. "Everything okay?"

She shook her head. "Fine."

He kissed her temple before standing up straight again to continue planning. "The stealth will only last until we board the ship, then it's all on us."

"Agreed, which means a smaller team would be better. Easier to slip by unnoticed. I would say… probably no more than five." Taln looked around her, as if judging each of her people to determine who went and who stayed.

"Well, I'm going," Cass said, wanting to cross her arms, but Kou's arm was in the way.

Taln looked over at her like she was a child butting into a *grownup* conversation. "We need people with more experience on this. Military experience preferred."

"You think I don't have experience? This is what I *do* for a living."

"I'm sure you may think so, but this is an entirely different beast. You're not prepared."

Cass jerked forward, but Kou's arm slammed into her stomach, holding her still. "There's a *reason* Surg hired me, and it wasn't to sit back and look pretty. I infiltrate ships for a living. It's all I do. It's all I've done for years."

"Yes," Taln said, not sounding convinced. "And you completely avoid conflict by essentially gassing the crew. Have you ever been in a fight?"

"Yes. You don't enter into piracy without expecting a fight from time to time. My way works well, really well, but it's not the only way. I know that." She nodded at the man behind her. "Kou knows I know that. I usually enter a ship with more tech and weapons on me than your average soldier."

"She does," Kou said, his words rumbling through her. "It's sexy as hacht."

She rolled her eyes, but was secretly pleased. "Now I know what to do to spice things up," she mumbled under her breath.

"What?"

"Nothing. You need me on this, if for no other reason than you'll never find her without my help. That's a large station. She could be anywhere, and we don't know where to look. Also, they're bound to have a lot of security."

"I know that," Taln said, stiffening. "I'm planning for it."

"But *I* can take it out of the equation. One beauty of being from an underrepresented species is that nobody's looking for you. I usually don't have a lot of problems with hacking other systems. I'm expecting their system to be more complex. It's a big company, lots of resources at their disposal, and they practically made a business out of making enemies and making friends with bad guys. You don't go down that route without being at least a little paranoid. Trust me, whatever you have planned, it probably isn't going to work."

Taln scoffed. "I've been planning this for years. I've studied *every* element of their security, *all* their security personnel, *all* their maps. There's not a thing I don't know about that station."

"And if you think that, you're a fool. There's a phrase on Earth, 'No plan survives first contact with the enemy.' I think you need to live that statement for a while. No matter how well you think you know that place, you don't. There's going to be something that surprises you. There're going to be situations that force you to improvise. There's no way around that. If you go into this thinking you know everything, you're gonna screw up. You're not gonna be prepared."

"And you know everything?"

"Fuck, no. Not even close. But I know I don't know everything, and therein lies the power. You can't look for solutions when you think you already have the answers."

"Lasses?" Angus said, cutting in.

"Yes, Angus." Cass leaned her ear toward the ceiling out of habit.

"We're here."

He walked confidently through the halls of the R&D section, moving toward his destination. Hours ago, a prisoner had escaped. He almost laughed, shaking his head instead. *Amateurs.* By the time anyone showed up at the cell to investigate, she was already long gone, her unconscious handler on the floor in a puddle of their own blood.

All he could say was he hadn't been involved yet. Not his problem.

Even so, ever since her escape, things had been going wrong. Random things. Lights going out, sensors going down. You name it.

He scoffed.

If upper management had thought to install more surveillance equipment in the secured laboratory wing, we wouldn't be here right now.

Not that anyone ever listened to *him* about such things. The R&D section held their most sensitive information, and no lowly "security guard," as some put it, had any business seeing what went on inside those hallowed halls.

But now, there was a rogue inventor running wild in there, and no way to find her. The exterior doors to that sector were among the most secure in the entire station, but once you entered, you had free rein.

Fortunately, she'd made one epic mistake… she'd messed with the station. He wasn't an engineer, so his eyes had started glazing over when they'd tried to explain what she did, but now they could track her. All they'd had to do was trace the modifications back to a terminal and game over.

They had her exact location.

He stepped up to the maintenance closet, lifting his pistol, which was set to stun. He nodded at the officer beside him. The other man smashed the locking mechanism and jerked the door open before spinning out of the way. The rest of them surged forward, but the space was small and tight. They could barely get two guns aimed through the narrow opening. There was no escape.

There was also no one there.

The map had been exactly what Victoria had needed. Once she'd studied it, she'd realized there was another corridor running behind the wall of the closet she'd been hiding in. The mesh walls opened easily, exposing the cables behind them, but from there, it got harder.

The cables had been wound tight, a complicated web that made it nearly impossible to get through. Without tools, her only option had been pulling and yanking on them in the hopes of making a large enough hole to see through.

With enough force, the ties holding them together snapped, but she had to be careful, afraid of disconnecting something important. The last thing she needed was to yank on the wrong cable and cut off life support.

When she'd pulled the cables out far enough to see through, her chest had tightened, and she'd slapped a hand against the wall blocking her way. She'd been hoping that maybe there was a passthrough, that the guts of the ship were accessible from either side, but no such luck.

She knocked on the wall. Her fist barely made a thud, almost absorbing the sound. Hope sprang up when she realized it wasn't made of metal. But that still meant she had to break through to the other side. "I am so not good at this," she whispered, pulling her fist back and closing her eyes. She punched her hand forward. The wall collapsed around her fist, scraping it raw. She pulled it back and held it. It was covered in dust and little bits of fiber from the wall. Several spots were cut and bleeding.

It'll heal.

But then her stomach growled. How long had it been since the last time she'd eaten? How long had she been in this closet? She held her fist against her chest, suddenly becoming worried. Though she rarely used her shifter abilities, it didn't change the fact that she was one. She could usually heal quickly and completely. Then again, if she was nutrient-deprived, she wouldn't heal at all. Shifting wasn't just a special power, it was an essential element in how her body functioned.

She was more careful as she widened the hole, using her good hand as she held the cut one against her heart. It was slow going, no more than a fistful coming out with each tug of her hand. It felt like hours by the time she stepped out into the new section, her calf scraping against the opening as she pulled herself through. "Damn." She looked down to check her leg, but it was too dark to see. The new corridor was pitch black.

"This is not good." She didn't exactly have a flashlight, and while she could change her eyes, make them more night adapted, they would still need light.

Her stomach growled again.

Then again, it won't matter if there's no light if I can't shift.

She rubbed her stomach. Shape-shifters couldn't shift if they were starving, something about lacking the energy to power it or something. But she wasn't there yet. At least, she didn't think she was.

Might as well try.

She concentrated on her eyes, a slight crawling sensation over-coming them as the passage lightened slightly, just enough to keep going. But a wave of exhaustion came along with it, and she wavered, banging her shoulder against the wall.

"Shit. This is not good."

Surg stood in Cass's cargo bay, feeling out of place. The space was filled with people girding up for battle. They talked back and forth, most of them unknown to him. Boots squeaked on floor panels. Guns were primed, a gentle whine filling the air as ammunition was checked. It was a bit of chaos, but somehow organized.

It all made him feel small, but he was determined to help, even if Taln was giving him dirty looks from her spot next to the airlock. She didn't want him involved, didn't want him coming along. She believed he would put everyone at risk. Maybe she was right, but he was also her boss, and she couldn't stop him.

Was she right, though? *Should* he stay behind? Was he putting the others in danger?

"Listen up," Cass said as she helped him don his body armor. "Have you used any of this shit before?"

He smirked. "I'm not generally in the practice of using shit." He was pretty confident that was a curse word, though he didn't know what it meant. Uso didn't have curse words.

"Quit being a smartass." She cinched something in place, causing him to grunt.

"Easy on the goods."

She rolled her eyes. "I think you'll survive." She checked his weapons before nodding in approval and stepping away, pointing him toward the airlock, where Taln and Kou were preparing a final briefing.

"Most of you are familiar with working under me. Those that aren't," she glared at Surg, "follow my directions *without* exception and without pause. Any delay could mean someone getting hurt or killed. Cass, what's the status on the hack?"

"We've got primary sensors and systems. Angus will inform me when we have full access."

Taln nodded. "That's enough to get started. All right, let's move."

CHAPTER TWENTY-EIGHT

*S*urg trailed behind Kou and Taln as they stepped through the airlocks into the station proper. It was eerily quiet, and they stopped at a signal from Taln. She leaned against a wall, peeking out around the corner.

"Relax, we're clear," Cass said behind him. "There isn't anyone in the corridors for another hundred yards in every direction."

Taln turned around and glared. "I have no idea what that means."

"Sorry. Coast is clear. The secured laboratories are to the left."

Taln nodded and stepped forward with her weapon raised, moving with silent grace. Surg felt like a baby animal by comparison, stumbling for its first steps. Still, he managed to stay quiet while two more of her team took up the rear.

They moved forward as one. Surg's heart pounded in his throat. He felt like he was going to be sick, but he kept moving, keeping his mind on Victoria, on getting her back to safety once more. That was all that mattered.

"Shit, wait," Cass said, stopping dead in the middle of the empty hallway.

Surg almost trampled her as he skidded to a stop. "What?" he whispered.

She stared at her right arm, running her left hand through her hair, dislodging several strands which fell across her face. "Victoria's missing."

"That's why we're here." He leaned over her shoulder, trying to see the display on her wrist.

She turned around. "No, I mean, they don't know where she is. She escaped. And they're looking for her."

"Anything?"

Eirse turned around as her boss glared her into oblivion. Like it was her fault the prisoner had escaped. She hadn't even *been* on that detail. No, she'd been called in once the woman disappeared. Now, she had to deal with panicked bureaucrats losing their minds.

"No, sir," she said, standing taller as she tried to keep her disdain from her face. It probably wasn't helping, but maybe he couldn't recognize it on a Tursiops's face. Most people had a hard time reading her kind. The Tursiops usually spent much of their lives in the water on their home planet. In the rare instances where they left, they usually preferred being in bodies of water. In fact, it was so rare to see them on dry land that sometimes people didn't even know what she was at first.

True, it probably didn't help that she was deformed. An accident had damaged her sails, making her little more than a cripple in the water. But on land? Totally different story. She was accustomed to moving when she had *water* holding her back. Moving through air was like… well… moving through air. It made her faster and stronger than the non-aquatic species she interacted with.

She tried not to think about how long it had been since she'd last been submerged. Or since she'd seen one of her own kind. Hell, she even tried not to think too hard about what she was expected to do here. She didn't agree with any of it, but it was a job, and it was as far away from her old life as she could get.

And what exactly has the job done for you?

Nothing, that's what.

"Find the girl," her boss snarled.

She nodded and turned her back on him. She didn't have a partner or team because she didn't play well with others, which was probably why she'd been relegated to this stupid space station for so long. What she wouldn't give for a little time in atmosphere, see a real body of water, breathe real air.

She touched under her arms where her sails should have been. After the accident, there'd been nothing left to fix. They'd been amputated, leaving her arms completely separated from her sides. It always felt weird. She always expected those flaps of skin to stop her when she lifted her arms, to feel that resistance, but it was gone.

Don't think about it.

"What's our status?" she said into her comm as she exited the security office. The hall was clear, empty. Of course, what prisoner would be stupid enough to hide out near the security offices? There was no reason to search here.

"Still no trace of her since the electrical closet."

She frowned and pulled the tablet out of her waist holder. Everyone was marking off where they'd searched, what was clear. There wasn't much left in the secured lab area to search.

Maybe because she isn't here.

She turned, heading back to the electrical closet. That was, after all, the last place they knew she'd been. If there was a clue, it would be there, wouldn't it? It was just two halls over. She sped up into a jog, her heavy boots beating a tattoo on the floor faster than her heartbeat.

Another thing I'll never get used to…

She slowed to a walk as she approached the closet. The lock mechanism was damaged when they breached. She pulled the door open. The metal was cool compared to most things. She liked it. The universe "on land" was often a little too hot for her kind.

And too dry.

Eirse scanned the room. It was tiny, the walls made of wire mesh. Behind them, a jumble of cables served to support the life of the station. "How did you get out of here without anyone the wiser?" She ran her fingers over the mesh, trying to come up with an idea.

It just didn't make sense. If she'd escaped through the halls, they would have found her by now. She was confident of that. Even an idiot could bungle their way into catching someone in the hallways.

Her eyes were better adapted to the dark than the other creatures on this station, though they didn't work as well in dry air as they did in water. Still, she opened section after section of mesh, looking for something out of place. Each section was neatly ordered and labeled, and she moved on quickly. Finally, she pulled back a mesh panel and found a jumble of tangled cables.

That *is not how the rest of the cables are organized.*

Someone had been through here.

Victoria couldn't see. She had no idea where she was, had no frame of reference to go by. The last inkling of light was back at that closet. She'd had nothing since. Now, only the cold touch of the walls, the gentle hum of the space station, the tap of her feet on the floor, and persistent pain guided her forward. Nothing else.

Because no one's following you.

Sadly, it wasn't as much of a comfort as she'd hoped.

She also was getting increasingly worried about her hand and calf. Her hand felt wet and rough from where she'd punched the wall. If she'd been in good shape, it would have been fine. It would have stopped bleeding by now, but it hadn't. No matter how many times she wiped her hand on her pants or shirt, it bled more. In the dark, she couldn't tell how much blood it was.

And that's not even the only wound.

Her hand didn't hurt that much, but her calf throbbed. It felt raw, and she could feel the blood running down the back of her leg. It wasn't healing either.

I'm going to die in here, aren't I?

She wanted to curl up and give in, but that wasn't an option. She felt overwhelmed, but she had to keep moving. In that way, maybe the darkness was a blessing, less information to distract her. Maybe then, she could keep her calm.

Except, I'm not healing.

She couldn't escape that thought. She could feel herself growing weaker, hungrier, more exhausted. It was getting harder to move. She was getting klutzy. She needed to get out of here.

Maybe they'll find me.

Except, how were they supposed to find her? She was in the walls. No matter where they looked for her, that was likely to be the *last* place they looked.

I'm gonna die in here.

Victoria leaned against the wall and slid to the floor. She breathed slowly, every breath feeling a little labored.

"They have to find me. They'll find me."

They'll find me.

CHAPTER TWENTY-NINE

*E*irse walked with purpose down the hallway, a plan in mind. There were only so many access points into that corridor. At least, unless the prisoner took a shortcut like before. Still, her best bet was to get ahead of the prisoner and cut her off.

Easy.

She jogged at speed, her long legs eating up the distance. She tried to ignore the pounding of each step against the floor, but it just reminded her of how her feet were currently confined, trapped, in those hellish boots. They were custom-ordered because the uniforms provided didn't include boots that fit her exceptionally long feet.

Yeah, "fit" is a stretch.

Her people usually separated their toes when walking on land, which gave them better balance. She'd refused to wear the boots at first, as they'd messed with her equilibrium. She'd been constantly holding the walls as her feet felt too narrow, too unstable.

Now, she was almost used to it. Still, it made her feet feel like they were being strangled, and she always looked forward to taking her shoes off at the end of the day.

She approached a door, slowing so it could open, and turned left, screeching to a halt when she nearly collided into another team. "Sorry," she said as she stopped, looking up, and froze in shock.

"You're not Diehli." She grabbed for the weapon at her side.

Taln stopped suddenly as the door to her right opened. She signaled the people behind her and satisfaction filled her as the sound of weapons warming up filled the corridor.

A tall person in a black uniform with striking teal skin came to an abrupt stop before her. "Sorry," the feminine voice said, a voice that rang like song. She looked up. "You're not Diehli." Her eyes were almost the same color as her skin, but seemed to glow, the enormous irises engulfing pinpoint pupils.

"Hands up," Taln said and nodded her head in concert with the command.

The woman lifted her chin, revealing parallel lines that might have been gills as her hands rose into the air. "You're insane."

"No. We're just looking for someone, someone your people took a few days ago."

"The prisoner."

Taln nodded. "Disarm her," she said to no one in particular.

A body moved around her, reaching for the weapon at the enemy woman's side. She didn't move, a confidence rolling off her that Taln found unendingly attractive in a woman. She

229

shook her teal head. "You guys are never getting out of here alive, even if you *do* find her."

"Oh, we'll find her. And even faster if you help."

She dropped her hands to her sides. "Why would *I* help you?"

Taln leaned in, not afraid of this woman for a moment, even though she probably should have been. There was something about her stance, her attire, or maybe it was those magnificently powerful thighs, that just *screamed* deadly. "Because the Diehli are monsters... and you're not." She leaned back, a smirk on her face.

The woman looked a little taken aback, but only for a moment before her expression closed up.

"You can either help us or not. You're not going anywhere, though. If you help us, we might be able to make it worth your while."

"I can't be bribed."

Taln shook her head. "Not a bribe. A job offer. And for a much better company."

She snorted. "You expect me to believe that?"

Taln angled her head toward Surg. "You see that man behind me? He owns Inia Intergalactic."

The other woman didn't speak, her expression carefully neutral.

"I'm Taln, by the way. And you are?"

She looked away, her chin obstinately tilted upward. "Eirse."

"Pleasure to meet you, Eirse. Now, where is she?"

Eirse stared at the wall, uncertain what to do. She'd heard of Inia Intergalactic. Who hadn't? Around Diehli, the company was called things like "interfering bastards" and "self-righteous pricks." If the Diehli were monsters, Inia were angels by comparison.

I don't deserve angels.

She'd sacrificed that a long time ago. You couldn't work this long for the Diehli without falling deeper and deeper down that dark abyss. Now, the Diehli was the best she could hope for. This was her life now. After the accident, she'd felt weak, useless. She'd thought she deserved no better.

Was she wrong?

Did she dare hope for more?

Eirse wasn't tied up, but being surrounded by the enemy was stifling. She was unarmed, and if they had lied about their intentions, she would be fish bait. No matter how skilled she was, she was just too thoroughly outnumbered.

And did she really want to fight? Certainly, Diehli wasn't worth it.

"So, where do we go?" Taln said, radiating confidence.

Eirse wasn't always great with interpreting the mannerisms of other species, especially land-based ones, but she could swear the woman was about to wink at her. "This way," she said, averting her gaze.

She supposed it didn't really matter in this moment what she thought of the Diehli or whether she considered Taln's offer. For the moment, their purposes were aligned.

They both wanted to find Victoria.

She could make the decision about double-crossing them later.

Surg trailed behind as the teal-colored woman led them through the hallways until they reached a maintenance access door.

"Through here," the woman said as she disengaged the lock and opened the door, exposing a dark corridor.

"Are there any lights?" Taln said as she leaned into the hole.

"One moment," Eirse said. She reached blindly into the opening, and after a little fumbling, a dim light illuminated the corridor for a short distance.

The light tinted everything orange, and Taln reached for her weapon, aiming it ahead of her. "Do you know if there's anyone else in here? Anyone we'd encounter?"

Eirse shook her head. "Not that I know of, but then I haven't checked in, so anything's possible." There was a smugness to her face as she spoke, like she half hoped the situation had changed.

But there was also an uncertainty, like she wasn't sure who she wanted to win this battle of wills.

Surg hoped she took the job offer. There was something about her that made him think she was quite capable, and Taln had always been a good judge of character. If she saw something in the woman, he would happily hire her.

And the more talent he could take from the Diehli, the better.

Taln turned and pointed at most of the group. "Stay here and guard this entrance. Eirse, Cass, and Surg, you're with me."

With a motioning of Taln's gun arm, Eirse moved through the doorway first, easily slipping out of sight. Next, Taln crossed through, then Cass, then Surg.

The corridor was narrow, forcing them to continue single file. The walls were lined with pipes and cables on racks, a monotonous display broken up by the occasional identifying tag. He felt almost claustrophobic as they continued step by step, the pronounced hum of the station closing in on him.

He started questioning why he came. They didn't need four people in this corridor. At best, they needed two. It wasn't like the people in the middle could be of much assistance if a fight broke out.

And there was an entire group of people waiting at the entrance, watching their backs. It was unlikely a fight would come from that direction, so the only direction to be concerned about was ahead of them.

They keep walking and time dragged on, unknowable and untrackable, as Surg's mind wandered. Before long, his worries for Victoria were bubbling back up to the surface. Would she be okay when they found her? Would she be injured? What had the Diehli done to her while in their custody?

"There's something up ahead," Eirse whisper-yelled. Immediately afterward, her boots pounded on the floor as she picked up speed.

Surg soon followed, but he couldn't see far enough to know what Eirse saw. "What is it?"

Eirse crouched down, and Surg waited impatiently for an answer. His hands fisted at his sides as he resisted the urge to pace.

"It's her."

"Well?" he said, frustrated at not being able to see her. "Is she okay?"

"She's unconscious."

"Move," Cass said, pushing Taln's shadowed form out of her way as she, too, crouched next to Victoria's body, which was seated against the wall, her head lolling against her chest.

Cass picked up Victoria's hand, examining it in the low light. "This isn't good."

"What is it?" Surg pushed forward, looming over Cass's shoulder. Taln had a similar stance behind Eirse on the opposite side of Victoria's limp form. He could just make out the abrasions and small cuts on Victoria's hand. They looked minor, inconsequential. "She looks fine. Why's she unconscious?"

Cass turned to look at him and shook her head. "You don't know shifter biology. This should have healed by now. If it hasn't, she's in bad shape. If things get bad enough, even something this minor can kill a shifter."

CHAPTER THIRTY

*S*urg didn't even remember the journey as they rushed back to the ship, his head ringing with Cass's words. They seemed impossible. How could a few cuts and scrapes be fatal? In the light of the main hallway, the wounds seemed even more minor, but they bled freely. In fact, he couldn't take his gaze away from the constant flow of red droplets that fell to the floor, creating a trail even an idiot could follow.

It didn't matter, though. This was almost over. They were almost to the ship.

"Shit. Bogies," Cass said as she looked down at her wrist.

"What's a bogey?" Taln hissed as she lifted her weapon.

"Enemy up ahead. By the airlock."

Taln nodded. "Cass, contact your ship. Alert everyone on board of the threat."

"Yes, ma'am," Cass said with a smirk, walking away slightly to make the call. After a few moments, she turned back around, smiling and forming a fist with her opposable thumb sticking straight up. He didn't recognize the gesture, but assumed it was a good sign.

"Let's go," Taln said. The others followed behind her. Eirse stayed back, Victoria in her arms, while Kou took up the rear, probably acting as rear guard while ensuring Eirse didn't run off with their target.

Surg lifted his own weapon as he took one last glance at Victoria's limp form. She looked unusually pale and lifeless. It was disconcerting, and he moved forward, taking a steadying breath.

"How many?" Taln said as she sidled up to the entrance and leaned her shoulder against the wall.

"About a dozen."

"Right. Everyone, take cover. Fire on my mark." She counted off on her fingers, then opened the door with her free hand. "Go, go, go."

The people closest to the door opened fire to provide cover, the sound exploding through the enclosed space. The others waited. When an opening in the fire occurred, the rest of them, including Surg, ran forward. There was nowhere to duck down. The enemy was waiting on the other side of the next door, using the frame as cover.

They all fired, and the air erupted in light and noise, drowning out all sense. Surg's heart pounded in his chest as he took aim and fired as well. The gun warmed with each pull of the trigger.

As he and his men rushed forward, the enemy's small hiding places became utterly useless. The doorframe and attached wall weren't large enough to protect them, and they fell quickly. His team stopped at the door, taking similar positions behind the doorframe, just inches from where a group of now dead Diehli had holed up.

Taln pushed to the front and leaned out, checking if the coast was clear. Cass had said there were a dozen men. As Surg looked down at the bodies near their feet, he saw at most half of that.

But once he looked, he couldn't look away. They were limp in a way that reminded him too much of Victoria's current state. The undeniable scent of cooked meat drifted in the air, causing his gaze to settle on the melted skin and clothing on the bodies.

Taln's fingers counted down again, and the hallway exploded into sound once more as the battle resumed. He detected movement in his peripheral vision as their team advanced, taking advantage of the cover fire. Another count, and the rest of them ran forward, guns raised, primed for carnage. Surg continued to fire to give them cover, and then finally, the corridor settled into quiet.

"Okay," Taln said as she motioned everyone forward.

"Airlock is good," Cass said, sticking her opposable finger in the air. Her gaze suddenly locked over Surg's shoulder, pain and guilt evidenced there.

Surg didn't need to turn around to know Eirse was bringing Victoria forward with Kou at her heels now that the shootout was over.

Cass stepped forward, touching him on the shoulder. "Don't worry. Shifters are pretty resilient. I'm not gonna let her die."

He nodded, but a part of him couldn't let go of his fear.

Victoria woke up to a familiar ceiling and sighed. She would recognize those panels anywhere. She'd picked them out herself.

Plus, she'd fallen unconscious in a pitch black corridor. Certainly, *something* positive had happened in the meantime.

Victoria didn't feel much better than she had before collapsing, though. She still felt weak, like her body was being sucked into the bedding. She doubted she could lift so much as a finger at the moment.

With great effort, she rolled her head to the side and smiled. Surg was sitting in a chair beside the bed.

"Victoria!" he said, jumping up from his seat. His entire appearance was a little rough and wild, but he rushed forward, latching onto her hands and holding them gingerly between his own. "It's good to see you awake."

She felt slightly dopey, and she wondered if it was the sappy moment, or if they'd given her drugs. "Good to be awake," she said. Her voice was faint and raspy, unrecognizable, but she didn't care. She'd escaped. She was free. And by the look in his eyes, Surg thought she hung the moon.

"You saved me?" she asked as the exhaustion started to take its toll.

"Me and a few others. You have good friends."

"Yeah, I do," she said with a smile. "You're good, too."

He leaned down and kissed the back of one of her hands. "So are you." He chuckled. "I can't believe you escaped. That was brilliant."

"I knew you would come for me," she mumbled as she lost consciousness again.

CHAPTER THIRTY-ONE

*S*urg, Victoria, Cass, Taln, and Kou had squeezed into the tiny cockpit to place a call with the other ships. The *Discovery*, *Areon*, and Varn's ship had continued following the signal of the stealth technology, and moments before, the *Trojan* had caught up. It was time for everyone to part.

Two windows popped up on the screen, one for each of the ships piloted by a person.

"Varn," Surg said with a nod as his brother's visage came up on the screen.

"You were successful?"

"Yes."

"I'm glad." His gaze shifted to Victoria. "In spite of everything, I hope you know I didn't want anything bad to happen to you."

She nodded, but turned to Surg in the seat next to her, looking puzzled.

Taln leaned over their shoulders, addressing her pilot on screen. "Prepare for docking with the *Trojan*."

"Yes, ma'am."

The team had spent the last few hours removing the stealth tech from the *Trojan* as they caught up with the other ships, much to Cass's chagrin. She'd griped and moaned the entire time, often saying things like, "Man, that would really come in handy." He would have barely noticed, except as soon as Victoria left medical, she'd sat back in a corner and smiled at her friend's antics, making him smile as well.

"Will you be joining me on my ship?" Varn asked, bringing Surg out of his thoughts. "I know you left your ship planetside at the beginning of all this mess."

He looked over at Victoria, a small smile on his face as she smiled back. "Not if Victoria wants me to stick around." He hadn't asked her yet. First she'd been ill and weak, taking nutrients first by a needle in the arm, then eating them normally. Then she'd seemed aloof, pulling away from the crowd, and he suspected after her ordeal, she'd needed the space to cope and adjust, so he'd given it to her.

They'd barely spoken since her return, though the few words they'd exchanged had been full of smiles and hope. At least, he was full of hope, hope that she would accept him, hope that he wouldn't be alone.

"That would be nice," she said in a faint voice, barely heard.

His smile grew, and he forgot about his brother on the other end of the call. His insides seemed to lighten, surging with energy as elation filled him. He wanted to jump to his feet, pick her up, and just spin around until they were both sick.

Varn cleared his throat, drawing Surg's attention once more. He looked uncertain as his gaze shifted between Surg and

Victoria. He opened his mouth to speak, then closed it, before finally speaking again. "Well, I'm going to continue after the stealth ship. We can't let that technology fall into the wrong hands."

"Thank you," Surg said with a nod, grateful for his brother, even if he suspected his sibling didn't understand his actions.

The call to the *Areon* cut off, and Taln spoke up again, "Varn, if I may, I would offer my ship in pursuit of the stealth technology."

"Thank you, Taln. That'll be greatly appreciated." He turned back to Surg. "Until next time, brother."

"Be safe."

"I will."

The window closed, and Cass spoke up. "Angus? Once the *Areon* leaves the airlock, pilot the *Discovery* into place so we can send Surg and Victoria on their way."

"Aye, Cass."

"Okay," Cass said, rubbing her hands together. "I guess we all need to make our way to the cargo bay.

Those who were sitting stood up, and they all filed down the colorful hallway until they stepped out into Cass's compartmentalized cargo bay. Already, the team Taln brought with her was waiting, checking their gear in their boredom.

"Prepare for docking. Loss of gravity imminent."

Everyone jerked to find a handhold as suddenly, the forces that were keeping them glued to the floor gradually released.

Somewhere, someone said, "Oh, this backwards tech is for the birds…"

"Hey!" Cass snapped. Her head swiveled around, as if she was looking for a victim to pulverize.

"Seal established. Airlock doors will open shortly."

Their feet quickly found the floor again.

Taln turned to Surg as the doors opened behind her. "Sir," she said with a nod.

"Taln," he said, nodding back.

Taln, her team, and Eirse slipped off the ship without fanfare, the door closing behind them.

Cass turned to them. "Okay, you guys next." Her smile faltered.

Kou wrapped an arm around her, squeezing her tight to his side. "Do not fear. You will hear from them soon."

She nodded and turned to Surg with an almost evil look in her eye. "You'll make sure she's safe? Make sure she calls?"

Surg suddenly felt like he was between a predator and her prey. He turned to Victoria, but he suspected she wanted nothing to do with this conversation. When the question of her safety had come up, she'd visibly paled, the color draining from her face. Surg turned back to Cass. "I can't make any promises for Victoria's actions, but I'll keep her safe, and I'll call if that will make you feel better."

Cass frowned, but nodded anyway.

Seemingly out of nowhere, Jessie came up and glommed onto Victoria. "I'm going to miss you so much."

Victoria looked to him with wide eyes as her arms flailed at her sides, locked in place by the near-adult's enthusiasm. She patted Jessie on her side as best she could. "I'll miss you, too."

Surg walked up and patted the near-adult on the shoulder. "Come on. Give her some air. I think her face is turning blue."

Jessie jerked back, her cheeks turning bright red, and mumbled an apology.

"The *Discovery* is in position," Angus said, interrupting the moment. "Are you ready to depart?"

Victoria nodded, and Surg offered his hand. She reached out and gripped his arm instead.

Cass stepped forward and hugged her. "Don't be a stranger."

They repeated the zero gravity bit, then the airlock doors opened once more.

As they walked through the doors and into the *Discovery's* laboratory, he couldn't keep his mind from running over Cass's words. Yet again, she'd insisted on a level of communication he wasn't sure Victoria was comfortable with. As the ships separated, he looked over at Victoria, watching as the tension left her body. This was her space, her home, maybe even her sanctuary.

She turned back to him. "Do you think I'm safe?"

"I'll keep you safe."

She rolled her eyes. "That's not what I asked. The Diehli are still out there. I doubt one failed attempt will dissuade them."

"If necessary, we can always go to Inia Intergalactic Headquarters. Even if they get in there, they won't find you."

"They've gotten in there before?"

"Yes, but they were quickly caught and stopped, and they didn't get to their target."

She nodded absently. "So, it's finally over."

"I'll make sure of it. Don't worry. You can finally get back to life as usual."

She smirked. "Well, not quite as usual. I used to live a very solitary lifestyle."

Everything froze up inside him. "Is that what you want?"

She shook her head. "No. I can't say I won't need my space from time to time, but I like having you around. We do well together." Her smile grew, and she leaned into him. "*Really* well together."

"That we do." He returned her smile, and his world finally felt right again.

After they returned to the *Discovery*, Victoria stayed in her lab while Surg disappeared down the hall, saying he had to make some arrangements. It felt strange with it all over, and she didn't know what to do. Her nerves hummed with the latent tension and stress of the recent crisis.

For a while, she just stood there, looking around the room, her happy place, as if she didn't even recognize it. It felt like it belonged to someone else, like she didn't belong here anymore. Everything looked the same. Every object was in its rightful place. She suspected it was her own eyes, her perspective, that was different now.

Victoria sat down at her workspace, staring at the equipment without really seeing them. She was hesitant to pull out her research. It was safe where it was, protected from prying eyes. She knew she would have to get it out eventually. Ship technology was her passion, her escape. She would go mad if she never returned to it, but she just couldn't seem to do it right now. She didn't feel like life had returned to normal yet.

And she worried. She worried that Surg was wrong, that the Diehli could find her and take her away again. She worried she would suck at relationships, that she would let Surg down. What did she know? She had three friends and those relationships would wither into dust if her friends didn't force the issue on a regular basis.

But there was a bigger issue at hand. She might have no practical experience with relationships, but she did know some things, like boredom, could foster resentment. Surg seemed happy to stay here now, but what would he do? He'd been a big time business person, which ordinarily would have terrified her, but she trusted him. He was a good person. But how could someone like that, someone with that much power, resign himself to living on a tiny ship full time?

She loved her ship, never really wanted to leave it, but she couldn't deny it was small. Tight spaces could make even the most loving couples end up at each other's throats. And what if after a while, she couldn't handle having someone living in such close quarters with her? She hadn't lived with anyone since moving out of Cass's home to live on the ship full time. What did she know about cohabiting?

Standing up, she wanted to pace. Her hands fluttered a little at her sides as the tension inside her built. She took a deep breath to try to calm herself, but like always, it didn't really help. She ran her hand over the countertop, letting the smooth feel of the surface settle into her bones, and that *did* help.

It wouldn't last, though. And she knew procrastination would only make this worse. The fears and anxieties would only build, and she knew at least some of them would be unfounded.

You can't solve a problem if you don't face it.

That was a hard pill to swallow, though. She kept her hand slowly running over the surface, her fingertips almost going numb from the repetitive motion, but it kept her grounded, thinking instead of focusing on how she felt.

"I have to talk to him." Forcing herself not to put this off, she took quick steps across the ship, almost running as she reached the hallway.

Surg turned in his seat as she reached the cockpit. "Victoria?" he said, sounding concerned.

"Everything's fine," she replied a little breathlessly. She took a deep breath.

Just do it.

But her words didn't want to leave her throat, and her mind went blank. *What do I say? What can I say?* "I... I wanted to make sure you'd be happy here."

He laughed, shaking his head, and her stomach sank. "Of course, I will."

"You don't *know* that," she protested, flinging her arms at her sides.

He stood, watching her for a moment as his hands rose as if to cradle her face. With a nod from her, he held her in both hands, his skin rough and warm against her cheeks.

She felt off-kilter and didn't really know what she wanted or needed.

"I have everything I need right here."

"But what about your business?"

"I can easily manage that here."

"You can?"

He nodded. "Besides, are you telling me you wouldn't take the ship to headquarters if I asked?"

"Of course, I would," she said, pulling back from his hands in outrage.

He smiled. "Besides, there are business opportunities right here."

She flinched, her old insecurities rising up. He was a business-man. Maybe this was just a ruse to get on her good side, to get at her inventions. "No, there aren't."

The look he gave her called her out on her lies, and she looked away, not able to maintain that connection. The truth was, she didn't really believe he would stoop so low. She really did believe he was a good man. She shook her head. "Even if I did perfect that technology, it wouldn't matter."

"Why not?"

She chuckled at herself. "I suck at business?"

"That's why you've got me," he said, leaning into her field of view.

She looked up at him, still hesitant, but on some level, she'd known this couldn't last forever. Running a ship, experiment-ing, inventing, living—it all took money. Eventually, the funds would run out.

"Let me ask you something."

"Yes."

He looked her in the eyes. "Do you trust me?"

"Of course, always."

"That's all that matters. Everything else is just details."

"Really?"

He nodded. "I'll follow your lead. If you want me to butt out, I'll butt out. If you want me to help, I'll help. If you want me to spread your inventions to the corners of the universe, I'll make sure it happens. Anything you want, I'll do whatever I can to make it a reality."

"That sounds a little one sided," she said, still feeling a unsure, but there was also this solid feeling building in her. It felt like, for the first time in her life, she wasn't drowning.

"You make me feel like I'm not alone. You make me realize that I've let certain things consume my life. You make me want to be a better person." He laughed. "And you do it effortlessly, just by being you."

She smiled, the last of her uncertainty slipping away. "Then it'll all work out, won't it?"

"Yeah, it will."

EPILOGUE

$\mathcal{C}$ass and Jessie were coming over to visit in a few minutes. Surg had talked her into it. Victoria was hesitant at first because she was very focused on her research right now, but it was Jessie's eighteenth birthday, and Surg had volunteered them to host the party.

With a sigh, she leaned away from her workstation and started cleaning up. She should have done so over an hour ago, but she wasn't always good at keeping track of time when she was in the zone. Turning around, she stopped at the assault of colors decorating her lab. "Happy Birthday, Jessie" was emblazoned on a banner across from the airlock doors so Jessie would see it the moment she arrived.

Across from Victoria, a table had been set up with drinks and junk food from Earth, while various party games from Earth were situated throughout the room. The tables looked a little odd, what with everything strapped down for gravity loss, but Surg had been pleased with the results. He'd done a lot of scheming with Cass and Angus for this, and had even talked her into a special trip to Earth to get supplies for this monstrosity.

At least, it was only going to be the five of them. Ellie and Zee were on a "super-secret" mission for the Ateles military, so they couldn't make it. Victoria was fine with this. She didn't like crowds and shuddered at even the thought of a party.

"Get ready," Angus said right before they lost gravity.

Once their feet hit the floor again, Surg ushered her in front of the banner and handed her some sort of party favor. She wasn't sure if it was a noisemaker or something intended to throw confetti, but she held it up at the ready anyway as Angus counted down over the intercom.

The door opened, and they both yanked on their favors, causing the air to erupt in colorful confetti as they said, "Surprise!"

"Oh my God," Jessie said.

Victoria couldn't quite see her through the cloud of paper.

"This is fantastic, guys. Thank you."

"Anything for my little sister," Cass said. The paper had cleared some, and she could now see Cass with her arm wrapped around Jessie, pressing their heads together in affection.

The party had gone on longer than Victoria would have liked, so she'd found a quiet corner to eat her cake in peace. The cake was covered in icing, a swirling monstrosity intended to look like a nebula. She stabbed her fork into the chocolate cake, avoiding the thick icing. It was like manna in her mouth. "Mmm…"

Around her, people were laughing and talking. Music played over the speakers. Currently, everyone else was playing the party games, having long abandoned the food table, which looked like it had been hit by a ravenous beast. It was almost empty, the cake little more than a shell of its former, magnificent self.

"There you are," Jessie said, sitting down on the floor next to her with her own piece of cake. "Done with the party?"

"I hope you enjoyed it."

"I did. It's great." She bumped Victoria's shoulder. "And you two make a great couple."

Victoria looked over, confused by the expression on Jessie's face. "What's wrong?"

She shrugged. "I don't know. It's just… since my sister fell in love, and Kou joined us…" She sighed. "It's just too lovey-dovey on that ship."

"Too small?"

"God, yes! It's bad enough my sister has always been a sex fiend. But now? Nowhere is sacred. I swear to God! The places I've found them going at it."

Victoria laughed. "I can only imagine." She and Surg were far more circumspect, and they had the ship to themselves. Personally, more than anything, she loved sneaking up and giving him a kiss. She liked surprising him, liked being in control of when they were intimate, but more than that, she loved seeing the look on his face when she did it. He always looked like she'd just given him his favorite thing in the whole world, like she'd made his day. Every time, she walked off, practically skipping down the hall, a giant grin stretching her face.

Jessie shook her head. "I don't think I can live with them anymore."

"What will you do?"

She shook her head again. "I don't know. Find myself?"

"Are you lost?"

"I don't know. Maybe. I just feel like an afterthought, an attachment."

"Then maybe you need to find your own place in the universe."

She looked over and smiled at Victoria. "Maybe I do. Have you?"

Victoria looked over at Surg and smiled. "I think I have."

READY FOR MORE?

This series will continue with Jessie in Shifting Tides.

Jessie was just tired of her sister's romantic antics. And envious. But during her bid for freedom, she unearths a terrible secret, a secret that will be kept buried at all costs...

Now Available for Pre-Order

GET 2 FREE EBOOKS

I love building relationships with my readers. As part of that, I regularly send emails with deleted scenes, never before seen excerpts, pre-order and new release announcements, and more.

If you sign up to receive these emails, I'll send you <u>Mila's Flight</u>, the prequel to the Darkest Day series, and <u>Shifting Sides</u>, the prequel to the A Shift in Space series, FREE.

Join Now to Get Your Free Ebooks

www.theeternalscribe.com

DID YOU ENJOY THE BOOK?

IF SO, YOU CAN MAKE A BIG DIFFERENCE...

Reviews are among the most important tools in my arsenal for getting my books in front of readers like yourself. I'm just one person. No matter how much I shout, my voice can only carry so far.

But do you want to know what does carry?

A crowd.

When one voice joins another who joins another, that matters. *That* gets heard.

Let your own voice be heard by leaving an honest review. It only takes a few minutes, but makes a major difference not just to me as an author, but to readers like yourself who are trying to decide on their next read.

Thanks again!

Danielle

ABOUT THE AUTHOR

Danielle Forrest is a Paranormal SciFi author and Medical Laboratory Scientist based out of Indianapolis, IN.

She has dedicated her life so far to two things:

Science & Books

So it really shouldn't be a surprise if science finds its way into even the most fantastical examples of her writing.

Sign up for her mailing list at www.theeternalscribe.com to get access to exclusive content and updates.

facebook.com/theeternalscribe

twitter.com/theternalscribe

instagram.com/theeternalscribe

goodreads.com/theeternalscribe

amazon.com/author/danielleforrest

bookbub.com/profile/danielle-forrest

ALSO BY DANIELLE FORREST

THE DARKEST DAY SERIES

Mila's Flight

Mila's Shift

Tristan's Choice

Terra's Fate

The Darkest Day Collection

A SHIFT IN SPACE SERIES

Shifting Sides

Shifting Cargo

Shifting Loot

Shifting Paradigms

Shifting Tides